Out of the sh...
the fire...

Thad winked at J...
here you thought...
who tells ice hockey players how to push a
puck around the ice."

"I don't think you're stupid," Janey said as
he slid off the stool and shut off the oven.

"You don't?" He slanted a questioning
glance at her.

Janey climbed off her stool and went to
stand next to him. "A stupid guy couldn't
have got me out of my clothes and into his
shower within the first fifteen minutes of
my arrival tonight."

Thad grinned as he leaned back against
the counter, folded his arms and gave her
the sexy once-over. "You do look rather
nice in my robe," he allowed in a low tone.

"And," Janey said recklessly, opening it
and letting it fall to the floor as her
romantic notions about Thad Lantz took
over full force, "I look even better
without it."

Available in August 2005 from Silhouette Special Edition

CATHY GILLEN THACKER

The Secret Wedding Wish

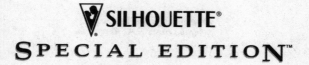

SILHOUETTE®

SPECIAL EDITION™

*First published in Great Britain 2005
Silhouette Books, Eton House, 18-24 Paradise Road,
Richmond, Surrey TW9 1SR*

© Cathy Gillen Thacker 2004

ISBN 0 373 75017 X

23-0805

*Printed and bound in Spain
by Litografía Rosés S.A., Barcelona*

Dear Reader,

From the moment of conception, a mother feels a fierce desire to protect her child and ensure that child's happiness. Guys love watching and playing and learning about sports. And therein lies the rub, because all sports carry with them the threat of disappointment and injury.

Janey Hart Campbell grew up with five boisterous brothers and she knows first hand how much joy athletics bring to growing boys. She has also seen the destructive side of unrealised ambition and crushed dreams and she fears her son's overriding interest in hockey is not just hurting his schoolwork and causing a rift between the two of them, but also taking him into dangerous territory…

The last thing professional hockey coach Thaddeus Lantz wants to do is get in the middle of a mother-son conflict, but when twelve-year-old Christopher pours out his heart to Thad and asks for his help, Thad can't say no. He makes it his business to talk to the feisty Janey. And as they say, life is never the same again…

I hope you enjoy *The Secret Wedding Wish* as much as I enjoyed writing it. For more information on my novels, you can visit my website at www.cathygillenthacker.com.

Sincerely,

Cathy Gillen Thacker

This book is for Jacob Talmadge Gerhardt.
Hero material. Definitely.
Welcome to the family, little one.

Chapter One

Janey Hart Campbell saw the Hart family posse coming as she turned the Closed sign in the window of Delectable Cakes. Knowing full well the last thing she needed was an emotional confrontation with all five of her very big and very opinionated brothers about her excessively sports-minded twelve-year-old son, Christopher, she ducked back out of sight of the old-fashioned plate glass windows and hightailed it to the back of her bakery. Grabbing purse and keys, she dashed out the back door, and ran right smack into the tall man standing on the other side of the threshold.

Immediately, Janey became aware of several things. The wall of testosterone she had just crashed into was a lot taller than she was. Probably six foot four or so to her five-foot-nine-inch frame. Not to mention all muscle, from the width and breadth of his powerful chest and shoulders, to his trim waist, lean hips and rock-hard thighs. He was casually dressed, in expensive sneakers, old jeans and a short-sleeved white cotton polo shirt that contrasted nicely with his suntanned skin. He smelled awfully nice, too, like a mixture of masculine soap and fresh-cut Carolina pines. His dark brown hair was the color of espresso, thick and curly, shorn neatly around the sides and back of his head. Longer on top, the three-quarter-inch strands brushed at the top of his forehead.

Individually, the features on his long, angular face were strong and unremarkable. But put together with those long-lashed electric blue eyes, don't-even-think-about-messing-with-me-jaw, and the sexy mustache that topped his sensually chiseled lips, the midthirty-something man looked good enough to put even someone like Mel Gibson to shame. More curiously yet, the handsome stranger was staring down at her as if he had expected her to come bursting out of her shop and run headlong into him.

"They said you were going to do this," he murmured with a beleaguered sigh.

Finally, Janey had the presence of mind to step back a pace, so there was a good half a foot of space between them. "Do what?" she demanded, aware her pulse was racing as she stood staring up at him.

He planted a big hand on her shoulder. "Run."

"And we were right, weren't we?" Dylan Hart said in the same know-it-all tone he used during his job as TV sportscaster, while he rounded the corner of the century-old building.

"Pay up," Fletcher Hart insisted, as he entered the alley that ran behind Main Street and sauntered up to the stranger.

"Don't forget. You owe me a beer." Cal Hart—who was still wearing his physician's badge from the medical center—grinned victoriously.

Janey glared at Cal. "Don't you have a surgery to perform or an athlete somewhere who needs your sports medicine expertise?"

"Nope." Cal smiled. "I'm all yours. For the moment, anyway."

"Great," Janey groused. Just what she needed after an entire day spent baking wedding cakes for this weekend's weddings.

Mac Hart shook his head at Janey. For once, he was without his Holly Springs Sheriff uniform and badge. "When are you going to learn you can't avoid your problems by running away?" Mac chided.

Janey folded her arms in front of her. Just because she had fled North Carolina once, in her teens, did not mean she was going to do it again. At thirty-three, she knew what she wanted out of life, and it was right here in Holly Springs, North Carolina—the town she had grown up in.

But not about to admit that to her nosy, interfering brothers, she sassed right back. "I don't know. Seems to me I've been doing a pretty good job ducking all of your phone calls."

"And look where it's gotten you," Joe Hart pointed out disapprovingly. Clad in running shorts and a T-shirt bearing the Carolina Storm insignia, her only married brother looked as if he had just come from one of his summer conditioning workouts.

The mystery man Janey had run into arched his

brow. "Maybe we should take this inside?" he suggested mildly.

"Good idea," her brothers concurred.

That swiftly, Janey found herself propelled out of the July heat and back into the air-conditioned comfort of her shop. To her consternation, the sexy stranger was still with them. Janey wrinkled her nose at him, wishing he weren't so darned cute. "Do I know you?" she asked cautiously, perplexed. Now that she studied him some more, he looked awfully familiar. Like she had seen him on TV, or in the newspaper, or a magazine, maybe. Certainly, he carried himself with the confident authority of someone used to being recognized and then thoroughly scrutinized.

Joe rolled his eyes in exasperation. "Oh, for Pete's sake! This is Thaddeus Lantz. Head coach of the Carolina Storm professional hockey team. The one I am now playing for!" he reminded her.

"Oh, yeah." Janey bit her lip as her eyes slid to Thad Lantz's and held. Now it was coming back to her. As well as the reason she had not wanted to recognize the savvy strategist.

DURING THE COURSE OF HIS coaching career, Thad Lantz had become used to all sorts of reactions to what he did. But never had anyone gone from the undeniable spark of mutual attraction to such utter loathing and suspicion so darn fast. And that was a shame. He hadn't ever been so physically drawn to a woman from the very first second they met, hadn't ever wanted to immediately take a woman into his arms, and into his bed.

Not that this was a surprise. Janey Hart Campbell was amazingly gorgeous and sexy, in the way that only a woman really coming into her own for the very first time could be. He guessed she was in her early thirties, a couple years younger than him. Her chestnut hair was thick, straight, and silky. He couldn't tell how long it was, since she had it caught up in a clip on the back of her head. But he was willing to bet at least shoulder-length. Her feisty amber eyes were framed by long lashes and delicate brows the same chestnut shade as her hair. She had a full lower lip, just made for kissing. A stubborn chin. And peachy gold skin. There was a dusting of freckles across her nose and a lifetime of knowledge in her woman's eyes. Lower still, were lush curves every bit as beautiful and tempting and feminine as her elegant, oval face. All in all, a very nice-looking package. Too bad, Thad thought with mounting regret, she only had heated resentment for him.

Janey turned to Joe. "You put him up to this, didn't you?" she accused.

Thad normally tried his best to stay out of family matters. This time he thought it best he intervene. He stepped forward, putting himself between Janey and Joe. "Actually, I'm the one who contacted your brother, Joe," he confessed kindly.

"And I'm the guilty party who summoned the rest of our brothers," Joe said.

Mac Hart, the oldest, looked at his younger sister

with compassion. "We understand why you feel the way you do, Janey, but this overprotectiveness of yours has got to stop," he stated firmly.

Dylan agreed emphatically. "Christopher has the right to choose his own particular path in life."

"Oh, for heaven's sake! He's twelve!" Janey protested in complete exasperation.

"And already thinking ahead to his future," Cal said proudly. "That's to be commended."

Janey folded her arms at her waist, the movement tucking her white cotton chef's jacket tighter across her full breasts and enviably slender waist. "Not if his thinking is leading him in the wrong direction!" she fumed.

"Who says it's the wrong direction?" the normally amiable Fletcher Hart scowled. "Bottom line is this, Janey. We are *not* going to let you turn that boy into a sissy!"

Janey's eyes widened in indignation. "Just because I want Christopher to concentrate on what's really important does not mean I'm out of line. And in fact, if anyone is out of line it is the five of you. Siccing the Hart Posse on me, indeed!"

Thad exchanged glances with all five of her brothers. Clearly, Janey was not going to listen to her brothers. "Maybe I should take it from here, fellas," he said amiably.

"Oh, no, you don't." Janey blocked the door before her brothers could take their leave. "You guys have something to say to me?" she stormed, color flooding her high elegantly boned cheeks. "You tell me right now!"

Joe looked his sister straight in the eye. "Why did you tell Christopher he can't attend hockey camp this summer?" he asked like the no-excuses professional athlete he was.

Janey's amber eyes turned even stormier. "Because Chris is enrolled in summer school to make up the math class he flunked last spring. And summer school is held at the same time as camp."

Sounded plausible, Thad thought, even as he tried to ignore the defensive note in her low voice.

"Did you even try to make other arrangements?" Cal asked.

"You're breaking his heart," Fletch concurred.

"You know, if it's really a question of cash that is preventing you from enrolling Chris," Mac volunteered quickly, "you could've come to any one of us and we would have been more than happy to help you out."

Janey's discomfiture turned to dismay. Suddenly it became very quiet as Janey asked very slowly and succinctly, "Where did you get that idea?"

All five Hart brothers looked at Thad.

Because he didn't want to embarrass her any more than she had already been, he reluctantly pulled the letter he had received—and shown—out of his jeans pocket and handed it to her. Janey's brow lifted quizzically. "What is this?"

"Read it," Thad said, knowing when she did she

would understand why the rest of them were so concerned about her son.

Janey folded her arms in front of her. "You read it."

"O-kay," Thad said, looking her up and down skeptically. "But I would think since you're his mother you would want to read it yourself."

"Oh, for pity's sake. Never mind!" Janey snatched it away from him.

"Dear Coach Lantz," she began reading out loud. "I think you are the best coach in the NHL and I want to come to camp so bad, especially now that my uncle Joe is gonna be playing for the Storm. But my mom says we don't have the money this year. And that's probably on account of my dad dying and us moving back here to be close to family. I know how hard my mom works, baking cakes, and I don't think she can work any harder. So what I was thinking is this. Could I maybe come to camp this year and then work off the cost for you by picking up towels or cleaning the locker room or mowing your lawn or something? I'd do anything. I just want to play. Sincerely, Christopher Hart Campbell. P.S. You can reach me at 111 Shady Lane in Holly Springs or by phone."

Her face pale, Janey let the note fall to her side.

Thad looked at her brothers. "I think I can take it from here," he told them confidently.

ALL FIVE of Janey's brothers filtered out. Janey looked as if she had never felt more mortified than she did at that very moment, and Thad could understand why. Her son had just done an end run around her, by taking a problem outside the family. Thad saw it as a sign he was growing up. Something for which Chris was to be commended. Janey seemed to think it was a sign she had failed her son, for not being available to him in the way Christopher needed her to be. She turned to Coach Lantz. Her peachy gold skin was ashen, her eyes turbulent with emotion.

"I don't know what to say except I'm very sorry my son put you in an awkward position."

"Don't be sorry," Thad advised. "Just fix it."

She held his steady, probing gaze. "Our situation is more complicated than it seems," Janey muttered at last.

"I'm sure it is," Thad agreed.

Janey regarded him suspiciously. "That's it? You're not going to try and convince me to let Christopher attend hockey camp?"

Thad shrugged, and decided to take the opposite approach of what she was obviously expecting. "You want to break his heart by denying him the opportunity to chase his dreams, that's your business."

Janey flushed at his blunt, matter-of-fact tone. "You don't understand the circumstances," she insisted.

Thad pulled out a chair at the white wrought-iron table in the corner. He sank into it and waited for her to do the same. "I know your late husband was Ty Campbell, and that he nearly made the US Olympic ski team."

Janey shook her head bitterly. "*Nearly* being the operative word."

"That's something to be proud of," Thad replied, stretching his long legs out in front of him.

Her eyes held such sadness as she sat down. "Being an alternate made my husband miserable."

"And by association you and Chris," Thad guessed.

'That's right.'

"Fortunately, we're not meeting to talk about your late husband. We're here to talk about your son." He looked at her sincerely. "I've got to tell you. I've been coaching hockey fifteen years now—and running camps during that time—and I've never had a letter like the one he sent me."

Janey shrugged her slender shoulders. "He's a resourceful kid."

"Obviously." As they both tried to get comfortable in chairs that were more ice-cream-shop-style decorative than utilitarian, their knees bumped. Rubbed. Pulled apart.

Janey dragged her thumb across the lacy scrollwork pattern on the table. "But he doesn't need to play hockey this summer to be happy."

Thad studied the defensive posture of her spine. "I don't think you can make that decision for him."

"Don't tell me what I can or cannot do, Coach Lantz!" She jumped up and began to pace the shop, her hips moving provocatively beneath the loose-fitting white cotton baker's trousers. "Chris is *my* son. I get to say if he plays hockey or not."

Thad tried not to think what her legs might look like. Were they as sexy and curvaceous as the rest of her? Struggling to keep his mind on the conversation at hand—instead of where this inherent attraction between them might lead—he turned his glance to her face. "And?" he demanded impatiently, irked with himself for getting sidetracked.

Janey gestured broadly with two delicately shaped hands. "And up until now I've allowed it."

"Because?" Thad prodded, curious as to whether her hands would feel as soft and silky as they looked, despite the fact she worked with them all day.

Janey folded her arms in front of her and regarded Thad stubbornly. "It wasn't skiing, or worse, the avalanche-skiing that led to his own father's death. Somehow hockey seemed a safer path—psychologically—to follow. But now it's becoming an obsession," she said worriedly.

Thad stood and closed the distance between them. "Maybe he's meant to go pro, like his uncle Joe."

"And maybe he's not. Maybe Joe's success has fueled Chris with false expectations and unrealistic dreams."

"So you're going to do what?" Thad queried in a dry tone meant to make her come to her senses and see how foolish she was being. "Deny him the opportunity to try?"

Janey gave him a measuring look. "Joe left home at sixteen. Did you know that?"

Thad was close enough to smell the deliciously sweet fragrance of vanilla and confectioner's sugar clinging to her hair and skin. "To play in the junior league up in Canada."

"Right. Mom wanted him to go to college and play there, if he wanted, on a university team. But Joe couldn't wait, so he did terrible in all his high-school classes and he begged and pleaded until Mom finally gave in."

"Not unlike most pro hockey players, I imagine. It's in their blood. And in their hearts."

"Which is fine, if they make it to the big time," she said, desperation in her eyes. "But if they don't. If they spend years chasing a certain vision and their dream never comes true, they become disillusioned and bitter."

"Not always," Thad disagreed. "Sometimes they become coaches."

Her lips parted as she looked up at him. "You—?"

"Tried to go pro. Didn't have the speed. So I took another path."

She leaned back against the display counter, her elbows propped high on either side of her. "You're the exception, not the rule."

Thad shrugged and tried not to notice how nice she looked in profile. "Chris seems pretty exceptional, too."

Janey turned her head to face him. "I'm not going to let him play hockey this summer."

"Your son has already lost a father," he reminded her calmly.

Janey stiffened, and swung all the way around to

face him. "So?" She squared off with him deliberately.

"So you don't think it'd do him good to be around a lot of positive male role models?"

She shrugged and assumed a look of extreme boredom. "Who also happen to play hockey for a living."

She was making a dig at his profession, too, but he refused to take the bait. "They're good guys. They share a common interest with Chris. And at his age, he needs to go out and mix it up a little bit, burn off some of that excess physical energy in a healthy, positive way."

Janey glared at Thad. "He does plenty of guy stuff as it is," she protested hotly.

"Such as?" Thad taunted softly, knowing if the subject weren't so serious he would really be tempted to seize upon the fireworks building between them and kiss her.

"Camping." As soon as the word was out of her mouth, Janey looked like she regretted it.

Which perversely made Thad want to take her in his arms all the more.

"*You* take him camping?" Thad ascertained, knowing bluster when he saw it, even if she didn't realize it.

"I'm going to this very weekend, as it happens," Janey boasted, looking determined to prove Thad and all five of her brothers wrong.

In for a penny, in for a pound, Thad thought.

"You'll see," she promised smugly, determination sparking in her pretty eyes. "This trip alone will provide Chris with all the summer adventure and physical challenge a boy his age needs.''

"Ah, please. She's not going to take him camping,'' Joe Hart snorted, as the waitress set down a pitcher of beer and a bucket of peanuts in the center of their table. Thad filled Janey's brothers in on the rest of his conversation with their headstrong sister. "The Great Outdoors isn't Janey's thing, never has been,'' Joe concluded.

Thad sipped his beer. "Well, *she* says they're going.''

Looking as at home in the bar as he did commentating sports events on TV, Dylan Hart tipped lazily back in his chair. "Did she say where?''

Thad nodded. "Lake Pine.'' It was a state recreation area, an hour or so away.

Mac Hart frowned and rubbed a hand across his chest. "The trail around the lake is easy enough, but it can be pretty miserable physically this time of year. Hot, muggy, uncomfortable.''

Fletcher Hart agreed. "Not to mention all the mosquitoes and chiggers.'' He shook his head. "Hope she remembers the insect repellent or they'll both be eaten alive.''

Cal took a sip of beer. "Isn't it supposed to rain tomorrow?'' he asked as he broke open another roasted shell and dug out the peanuts inside. "Sunday, too?''

Joe scowled, obviously still as peeved as Thad at the way Janey refused to support her son's athletic ambition. "Maybe that's what she needs, a little bad experience at Lake Pine to make her feel that a few turns around a hockey rink aren't such a bad deal after all." It certainly hadn't been for Joe, who was in the midst of a successful pro hockey career.

Thad knew Janey's brothers had a point. There was no more potent teacher than experience, particularly bad experience. On the other hand, he had been caught out in foul weather, with only camping gear to protect him. It wasn't an experience he would wish on anyone else. Particularly if there were thunderstorms, a hopelessly headstrong woman, and twelve-year-old boy involved. "You can't seriously think she would head off with a backpack and tent if bad weather is brewing," Thad said finally.

The Hart brothers exchanged glances and shrugged. Finally, Cal spoke for all of them. "She might if she were hell-bent on proving a point. Not that it really matters. Ten to one, if it does rain, they'll end up in the park lodge before nightfall."

It wasn't his business, Thad told himself as he left. If Janey's brothers were willing to let her tough it out and make her own mistakes, he surely ought to be able to do the same. Especially if the ultimate result was Janey letting Chris pursue his dreams. But even as Thad pushed the problem from his mind, an image kept coming back of a tall slender woman with thick chestnut hair and amber eyes.

Chapter Two

"Are you sure you want to do this, Mom?" Chris asked, as Janey lugged the sleeping bags and backpacks out into the living room.

For the tenth time that morning, he walked over to the telephone answering machine and checked to make sure there were no new messages. "I mean, camping out was never your thing. It was something Dad and I did." His face took on that pinched look it got whenever his father's name came up.

The guilt she had been feeling ever since he'd begun asking to go to camp intensified. Her son might be only twelve, but he was growing up so fast now. And she wasn't just talking about the growth spurt he'd been undergoing that had him—at five foot ten— standing an inch above her and left his gangly arms and legs looking too long for his body. His face was undergoing changes, too. Oh, he still had the dusting of light brown freckles across his sturdy Hart nose, and Janey's stubborn chin and Ty's deep blue eyes, but his boyishness was fading. In its place was a hint of the strong and gutsy man he would become. "I'm sorry I haven't taken you," Janey told him sincerely.

"That's okay." Chris rushed to reassure her, as he straightened the Carolina Storm cap he wore overtop of his close-cropped chestnut hair, with the brim turned to shade the back of his neck. Chris looked at Janey with enough understanding to break her heart. "I know you've been real busy. And that money's tight right now."

"Not that tight," Janey said, trying to shake off a pang of guilt. Maybe that's what this whole got-to-play-hockey-to-live thing with her son was about. Maybe he just wanted her attention. Wanted to somehow fill the void in his life left by his dad's death two years before. Janey had assumed that Chris had worked through his grief, just as she had, and accepted the fact that from now on it was going to be just the two of them. But the fact Chris had elevated Thad Lantz to hero status—and then reached out to Thad in such a personal, unexpected way—told her that was not the case.

Her son wanted a man in his life he could hero-worship the same way he had Ty. For reasons unbeknownst to Janey, Chris had bypassed all five of his uncles and selected Thad Lantz to fit the bill. A fact that put her in a very awkward situation, the physical attraction she felt for Thad notwithstanding.

"What about our mail?" Chris worried out loud, looking out the window at the black mailbox next to the curb. "What are we going to do about that?"

"We can get it tomorrow evening, when we come back home," Janey promised.

Chris looked even more pained.

"I'll just check, and make sure there isn't anything out there now," he said, racing out the door and down the sidewalk.

Watching him open the metal lid, Janey sighed. She knew what he was looking for—a response from Thad Lantz.

Which was another reason she had to get her son out of town. She wanted Chris to be in a positive frame of mind when she explained to him why he couldn't go to summer hockey camp this year. And she didn't want any of her brothers around when she did so.

Chris peered at the sky a short while later as they lugged their gear out to the minivan. It was light gray, with darker clouds here and there. "Kind of looks like rain."

"I looked at the weather radar when I got up this morning," Janey reassured him. "The storms are supposed to hit well east of Lake Pine. We should be okay."

THAD HAD NO PLANS for the weekend, but figured he might as well enjoy his time off while he could. So he booked a room at the lodge at Lake Pine, figuring if the weather held he could rent a boat and take it out on the lake and do some fishing, and if it didn't, well, the restaurant there was fair, the view scenic.

And as long as he was headed out that way, he figured he could do the Sir Galahad routine, if necessary.

By the time he was halfway there, the skies opened up. It was still raining cats and dogs as he turned his Lincoln Navigator in to the deserted parking lot of the campsite registration center late Saturday afternoon. Thad wasn't surprised to see the flat-roofed concrete building was empty except for the uniformed park ranger seated behind the desk. If it weren't for his prickling conscience—the feeling that his actions had somehow goaded Janey Hart Campbell and her son Chris into an ill-scheduled backpacking trip—he wouldn't be here, either.

"Hi, I'm Thad Lantz." He held out his palm.

"Coach for the Carolina Storm. I recognize you." The ranger, a clean-cut man in his late forties shook hands with him. "Hell of a run the team made last year. Think you'll make it to the Stanley Cup this year?"

Thad smiled, relieved to meet a fan. He rarely played on his own celebrity. Today was the exception and he would use it to the hilt.

"One can hope. Which in a roundabout way is why I'm here. Family of one of my players are supposed to be backpacking here this weekend. Janey Hart Campbell and her son Christopher. Given the ugly turn in the weather, there's been some concern." And all on my part, Thad added to himself. "Since I was on my way out here, I volunteered to check up on them, make sure they were okay."

The ranger hesitated. "Normally, this isn't the kind of information we'd give out, you understand."

Thad nodded soberly. Normally it wasn't the kind of information he would be asking for, either. But something about Janey Hart Campbell's vulnerability had gotten to him yesterday. And he had seen, first-hand, just how stubborn, fiercely independent, and single-minded she was. Plus, he knew the fact she and her son were here at all today was probably his fault, for letting his conversation with her end without some sort of solution to the sticky situation. And that was unlike him, too. He was a take-charge kind of guy. Used to handling all sorts of people. He should have insisted he be able to talk to her son, even if it was only to tell Chris gently there was nothing he could do for him about hockey camp this year. But he had let the problem linger on because he had wanted a reason to see her again.

"But under the circumstances I guess I can tell you they were in here about three hours ago and headed out on the trail," the ranger continued.

As Thad had driven closer, he'd seen the torrents of rain pounding the area. "Did they have enough time to get to their assigned campsite before the rain hit?" he asked hopefully.

The ranger shook his head. "It's a good four-hour hike, without packs. And it started raining about an hour and a half ago."

"Is there any way to check, without hiking it my-self, to make sure they're okay?"

"We don't take jeeps out on those trails unless it's an emergency, and right now, without any lightning or thunder—"

The door opened behind Thad. He and the ranger turned simultaneously. "Well, speak of the devil." The ranger grinned. He nodded at the drenched Janey and her son Christopher, as they unbuckled their harnesses and set down their packs.

They couldn't have been any wetter had they jumped into the lake for a swim. And yet, Thad noted, Janey still looked amazingly beautiful. Even with soppy wet clothes, drenched hair and exertion-red cheeks.

"Coach Lantz here was looking for you two."

Janey briefly caught Thad's eyes while her son stared at him, agog.

"I bet I know what you want to talk to me about, too," Chris said, immediately excited as a pained expression crossed Janey's pretty face.

Before her son could say anything else, she turned her back to Thad.

He had been wondering the other day about her legs. No more. As he got his first look at them, he noted they were as shapely and feminine as the rest of her. The skin was silky smooth and lightly tanned beneath the hem of her knee-length walking shorts. Her ankles were trim, too, in slouchy socks, her dainty feet encased in sturdy albeit quite wet and muddy hiking boots.

He had a very nice view of her derriere as she

quickly asked the ranger, "Is there any way we can get a ride back to my van? It's at the other end of the hiking trail."

The ranger checked his watch. "The shuttle will be by in another forty minutes. Because you got rained out, you can apply your campsite fee to a lodge room rent for the night. I can go ahead and do that for you now, if you want, on this computer."

"Can we, Mom?" Chris asked eagerly.

Janey seemed to be torn between wanting to just go home, and wanting to keep her promise of a weekend getaway to her son.

"When the weather turns bad like this, the lodge fills up fast," the ranger warned.

Janey glanced at her son. It was clear that Christopher wanted to stay. She turned back to the ranger. "Sure," she said, although Thad noted her cheerful smile seemed forced. "We appreciate it."

"Happy to help." The ranger typed in several commands. He tore off a slip and handed it to Janey. "Just give that to the front desk when you check in."

"I can give you a ride," Thad said casually.

Janey looked stunned by his chivalry. "To my minivan?"

"Or the lodge first. Wherever you want." He didn't know why it mattered to him. He wasn't the kind of guy to assume anyone else's personal troubles, especially those involving someone else's child. But he couldn't just walk away and leave Janey and her son sitting there, like two drenched rats, when a lodge room with a warm shower and hopefully dry clothes was a mere ten-to-fifteen-minute car ride away.

"That settles it then," the ranger said as the phone behind his desk rang.

Thad opened the door. Janey hesitated for only a moment, then swept through.

JANEY COULDN'T BELIEVE she had run into him now, of all times, when she was looking like a wet dishrag! Not that it was an accident. Clearly, he had come here looking for her and Chris. At the behest of her brothers again? Probably. She didn't know why but that rankled more than if he had just come searching her out on his own.

Not that she was the least bit interested in him. Ruggedly attractive or not, he was the kind of man she needed to steer clear of.

"Sorry your camping trip was cut short," Thad remarked as he hit the keyless entry pad and unlocked the door to his big Lincoln Navigator.

"We don't mind. Do we, Mom?" Chris gave Thad yet another adoring glance as he headed for the right rear passenger door and jumped in.

Janey was about to follow him when Thad stepped ahead and opened the front passenger door for her.

"Let me take that for you." He relieved her of her heavy backpack and the additional nylon food bag and camp stove.

Janey slid in, while Thad stowed her gear in the cargo area, behind the seats. Leave it to her to get stuck with a man who was so well-liked and respected within the community she would be hard pressed to find fault with him.

"This is so awesome!" Chris said as Thad slid behind the wheel. Unlike Janey, Thad was barely wet, and looked handsome and pulled together in khaki slacks, dark blue knit sport shirt and lightweight windbreaker. Just like before, he smelled like a mixture of masculine soap and shampoo and fresh-cut Carolina pines. Another shimmer of awareness sifted through her.

"'Cause I've been wanting to talk to you, Coach," Chris continued exuberantly, leaning forward in his seat. "You probably don't know this but I wrote you a letter about going to your camp, seeing if I could get some sort of scholarship or work to help me pay for it—"

Thad looked at Janey, as well aware as she that thanks to her insistence on cutting their meeting short, nothing had been decided yet.

"Actually," Thad told her son, as guilt flowed through Janey anew and he turned around to face Chris, "that's why I was looking for you and your mom today. I did receive your letter. And I knew it was something that should be discussed."

Chris's face lit up like the sky on the Fourth of July. "Did you hear that, Mom? He's gonna let me go to camp, even if we can't pay for it all up front. Isn't that great?"

Janey knew nothing of the kind had been promised. Just as she knew she hadn't seen her son looking so excited about anything since...well, since never. He had been through so much. Losing his father. Moving cross-country. If playing hockey helped him get past the last of his grief, and feel real joy again, who was she to deny him? "Actually..." Janey took a deep breath. "You don't need a scholarship, Chris. I've taken care of that." Or I will soon, she amended silently. "And you can go to summer hockey camp next week on two conditions. First, you get permisson from your summer school teacher and are able to get an excused absence from your math class. And second, that you do all the makeup work!"

"No problem," Chris enthused, making the victory sign with his fist. "I'll talk to her Monday, first thing."

"Camp starts one week from tomorrow, and runs through the following Friday afternoon," Thad said.

Chris beamed, looking like every wish he had ever dreamed had just come true. "This is the best summer ever!"

Janey only wished.

"I'M TRYING TO AVOID being recognized again. What's your excuse?"

Actually, Janey had been trying to avoid running into Thad Lantz for fear of hearing him say "I told you so" or something similar. Not easy in an establishment the size of the Lake Pine Lodge, where there was only one restaurant and lounge.

"What can I say? I can't get enough of the rain," Janey fibbed, as she leaned back against the side of the building that fronted the terrace, watching the rain pour off the overhang in sheets. There was just enough room for the two of them to stand there, side by side, without being seen or getting wet.

"Now why aren't I buying that?" Thad murmured, moving closer yet.

Because it's not true, Janey thought, taking a sip of scalding coffee, laced with both brandy and cream. She tried desperately to ignore his tall, broad-shouldered silhouette and warm herself up. Since coming in off the trail, she had taken a long hot shower and dressed in the warmest clothes she had with her—a long-sleeved yellow T-shirt and pair of olive green hiking shorts, knee socks, and her now cleaned-up boots. She had used the hotel blow-dryer to dry her chestnut hair, but because of the nature of the trip she'd had no styling products to put in it, and the continuing humidity had it curling wildly and uncontrollably to her shoulders.

Not that Thad Lantz seemed to mind. The ruggedly handsome coach was staring down at her as if she were the loveliest creature on earth.

Janey did her best to contain another shiver as she took a second sip of coffee and tried not to think about how deep down she had been secretly hoping she'd be forced to talk to Thad again this evening, despite everything.

She tilted her head at him, noticing how masculine and at ease he looked in the glow of the terrace lanterns. He was wearing the same clothes he'd had on earlier—minus the windbreaker, of course—but it looked as if he had shaved again. Ran a brush through

his own naturally curly hair, and somehow tidied—
or trimmed—his dark mustache. If she didn't know
better, she'd think he was on the prowl for some romance himself. But men on the prowl for romance
didn't hide on the outside terrace in the rain on a dark
and stormy July evening.

Wondering if his hair would feel as silky and thick
as it looked beneath her fingertips, she turned her
glance away and concentrated on her coffee. She
wished he would quit contemplating her as if he
wanted to kiss her. Wished she would quit wanting
him to. Just to satisfy her considerable feminine curiosity, of course, since she had never been kissed by
a man with a mustache.

"Don't you have something better to do?" she
asked wryly.

He shrugged and his smile widened as he spoke in
a low, sexy voice that did funny things to her insides.
"Don't you?"

So much for shooing him away.

For the first time Janey noticed he had some coffee
with him, too. Irish, if her nose was telling her cor-
rectly.

He took a sip as he eyed her seriously. "Where's
Chris?"

"Video arcade." Was it her imagination or was
this terrace getting smaller by the minute? She swallowed around the sudden parched feeling in her throat
and tried to pretend being alone with him like this
didn't bother her in the least. "Since the storm
knocked out all the cable TV for the evening, and the

kids can't swim or play on the tennis courts due to the rain, the management gave the kids free tokens to use.''

Deciding she was much too close to him, she backed up a step.

He smiled at her as if reading her thoughts, but stayed where he was, lounging against the rough-hewn log wall of the lodge. "Chris must have liked that.''

"Oh, yeah." Janey warmed at the caring in his voice. "There are probably fifty kids down there."

He turned, so his shoulder was bracing the wall, and let his glance drift lazily over her. His smile broadened as he returned to her eyes. "Enough machines?"

Janey's heart skipped a beat at the sexual awareness shimmering between them. She hadn't wanted anyone in such a long time. She didn't know what to do with the yearning. "They've got a couple of busboys down there, running some sort of competition and keeping order." Everyone had seemed very happy when Janey left to find amusement for herself—or was it really distraction from all her ridiculously uncalled-for, unexpectedly romantic thoughts?

He drained the rest of his coffee, then set the empty mug on one of the tables to the left of them. "You made the right decision—letting Chris go to camp after all.''

"Yes, well…"

He went back to leaning against the building, his muscular arms folded in front of his solid-looking chest. He studied her with narrowed eyes, then ascertained gently, ''But you're still not happy about it, are you?''

That was putting it lightly, Janey thought. Chris was so much like his father. Ty's unrealized athletic dreams and the resulting bitterness had poisoned Ty's soul, as well as his marriage to her. The only saving grace had been Ty's love for Chris, and his determination to shield his son from his own shattered hopes. She didn't want Chris's thwarted goals or frustrations in that regard poisoning their relationship, too. But she knew, with the odds against actually achieving the kind of pro career Chris dreamed about, that it was a definite possibility if he started on this track and did not get where he wanted. But loath to get into all that with Thad, she said simply, ''He still has to get permission from his summer school teacher.''

Thad continued regarding her seriously. ''I imagine that can be arranged.'' He edged closer. ''I've been thinking about what you said, though. About your brother Joe's stardom giving Chris unrealistic expectations of his own.''

''And?'' Janey drained her mug and set it aside, too.

''All kids his age have stars in their eyes. But there's a way to bring him back to earth.''

''I'm listening,'' Janey murmured.

''He wanted to work off his tuition anyway, right?''

Janey nodded.

''So let him work at the practice facility, picking

up towels and stuff in the locker room, for an hour or two every day. Let him see how grueling and demanding the sport is for professional hockey players.''

"I agree that would definitely help, in that regard.'' Janey bit her lip uncertainly as a gust of rain-drenched wind blew across them, making her shiver.

"But?" Thad prodded, as he reached up to brush a strand of hair from her face and tuck it behind her ear.

Tingling all over from just that light casual touch, Janey shoved her hands in her pockets and tried not to think how it would feel to be held against that broad chest as she turned her face up to his. "How is being around all those jocks going to help him stay serious about his schoolwork?"

Thad gave her the slow and tender once-over. "I'll talk to him, tell him how much I learned playing on a college team. And I'll have the other players who went the university route talk to him, too."

"Thanks."

"So does this mean we're not enemies anymore?" he teased, his electric blue eyes twinkling.

Janey's mouth dropped into a round O of surprise as she fortified herself against the sexy mischief suddenly in his eyes. Sensing that this commanding coach could be dangerous to her heart if given half a chance, she unlocked their gazes, vowing she would not let this shift into a flirtation. "I never said—"

"Didn't have to," Thad murmured, coming so

close she couldn't help but inhale his clean, pine-scented fragrance.

"I know your type," he informed her softly as he wrapped both his arms about her waist, and guided her close.

"And that is?"

He lifted her hand to his lips and pressed a kiss to the back of it, sending another tingle of awareness arrowing through her. Still holding her eyes with provoking gallantry, he said, "You *think* you want Mr. Sensitive."

Janey's heart raced as her arms flattened against his chest, holding him at bay. "I hardly find anything wrong with that."

"When what you really want is a Real Man."

Janey did her best to smother a laugh. The one thing she never had been able to resist was a sense of humor. "And what category are you in, pray tell?" she teased right back.

"Kiss me," Thad urged huskily, his head already lowering as he looked deep into her eyes. "And see."

Chapter Three

Thad hadn't planned this. He knew it would have been better had he not gotten involved with Janey Hart Campbell at all in a personal way, but there was just something about her that kept him coming back for more, that had him wanting to take her in his arms and kiss her passionately from the very first. And now that her soft lips were beneath his, and he could feel the sweet surrender of her body melting into his, there was no stopping with just one kiss, no pretending something incredible wasn't happening between them. Planned or not. Passion like this came along once in a lifetime—*if* you were lucky. And though instinct told him that Janey hadn't been well-loved in the past, Thad knew that was something he could easily change. All she had to do was give him a chance. And he would show her how wonderful an unscripted liaison like this could be.

Janey had figured Thad's mouth would be warm, his kiss as sure and utterly sexy as the rest of him. What she hadn't counted on was the way it would make her feel—reckless and wonderful. Or how she would react to the silken warmth of his lips, the sheer male insistence of his kiss, the invasion of his tongue. She'd expected to resist his advances a lot more. After all, it had been years since anyone had wanted her like this, since she had even considered allowing something as simple as a kiss. And yet the moment he took her into his arms, and gave her a long thorough kiss meant to shatter her resolve, yearning swept through her in sweet, wild waves. Her middle fluttered weightlessly, and her knees trembled weakly as heat worked its way through each and every inch of her. She had been married, she'd had a baby, but she had never been kissed or held this way, like she was the most precious woman in all the world.

It was a sensation Janey feared would be all too easy to get used to, a feeling that could just as easily be taken away. And right now, Janey'd already suffered all of life's disappointments she could handle. Shaking, wary of giving her heart away much too easily, she drew away. Looked up into his face. Her only comfort, the fact he looked as stunned and overwhelmed by what had just happened between them as she was.

The terrace door opened.

As Janey got a good look at the person interrupting them, it was all she could do not to groan out loud. Of all the lousy timing…

"What?" Thad asked, still looking mesmerized by her, instead of the interloper about to join them.

"See for yourself," Janey muttered as Thad reluctantly turned away from her and came face-to-face with Janey's eldest brother. Darn it all. She should have known her family wouldn't be able to let her be for long.

"Well, my first question is answered," Mac said, looking like he wanted to punch Thad out but good. Mac turned back to Janey, looking as much a law-and-order man as ever, even without his sheriff's uniform. "You are here. And you're safe from the elements." Mac swept a hand through his close-cropped dark hair and scowled at Thad. "I'm not so sure about the rest—"

"Mac, please." Janey held out both palms, in a staying gesture. "This is not the time to go all protective on me." She was so tired of her brothers doing that!

Mac stepped beneath the overhang. He positioned himself between Janey and Thad and scowled from one to the other. "It looks like the perfect time to me."

Janey pushed past Mac. She took Thad's hand in hers and rested her face against his shoulder. "I know what I'm doing," she insisted stubbornly. Even if Thad—who had gallantly followed her lead and encircled her waist with his arm—didn't. Yet.

Mac arched a skeptical brow. "Do you?" he ground out, his look reminding Janey of all the times she had behaved recklessly in the past to prove a point with her smothering, overprotective family, and then regretted it later.

"I think your sister has a point," Thad interceded,

tightening his grip on Janey as possessively as if they had something passionate and enduring going on between them to defend, instead of just a simple, highly experimental, flirtatious kiss. "She is a grown woman. A savvy businessperson, as well as a mother."

"Oh, my Lord." As Mac stared at them, his face began to lose color.

"What?" Janey said, wondering what completely unfounded conclusion her eldest brother had jumped to now.

Mac gave her a frank, assessing look as rain continued to pour down from the sky in heavy sheets, just to the left of them.

"You haven't..." Mac said with a telltale lift of his brow. "Please. Tell me you're not..."

"Not what?" Janey demanded impatiently.

"Trying to work off Chris's camp fees that way, are you?"

Mac was teasing, Janey saw finally.

And he wasn't.

"Very funny," Janey said stiffly, irritated her brother could even hint she would be irresponsible enough to use her femininity on some unsuspecting man to get her way. "And no, I am not."

Now it was Thad's turn to look as if he felt like punching someone out on Janey's behalf, Janey noted. She felt oddly pleased as Thad stepped protectively in front of her. "If you weren't her brother," Thad warned Mac, "you'd be eating a knuckle sandwich about now."

No less on guard, Mac shot Thad a warning look. "I'm glad you feel that way," Mac stated bluntly. "Because if you didn't want to defend her honor just now that would really say something about your character or lack thereof."

"Remind me to tell you about the 'tests' my brothers put all my prospective beau through." Janey pushed out the words through tightly gritted teeth. Older or younger, it hadn't mattered. All five members of the Hart posse had been perfectly capable of saying the wrong thing at the right time to ensure her romances with the guys she dated before Ty went absolutely nowhere. And Janey knew now what she had realized then—that her siblings' "interruptions" and "interferences" had been as well planned as they had been executed.

"Make fun all you want," Mac told her smugly. "But they worked, didn't they? No one tried to take advantage of you as long as the five of us were around." It was only when she had gone off to Colorado, on spring break with her friends, that she had gotten herself into trouble by getting involved with Ty. And Janey knew her entire family still felt that wouldn't have happened if they had been nearby to stop it.

Mac looked back at Thad and continued with a candor that was serious now and strictly man-to-man. "Listen, I know my sister comes off as headstrong and impetuous, and I'll be the first to grant she has a wild streak a mile wide. But bottom line, she's a lot more innocent and naive than she seems at first look.

None of us want to see her hurt. And I am speaking for every one of her brothers, as well as her mother now."

It was official. Janey felt as if she were back in high school. No. Make that junior high.

"I understand," Thad told Mac soberly as the two of them shook hands. "And I have no intention of hurting her."

Janey felt like stomping her foot. "Excuse me. I think I *might* have something to say about this!" Janey interrupted, mortified.

Oblivious to her upset, Mac looked back at her. Now that he had extracted the chivalrous agreement from Thad, Mac was ready to move on to other subjects. "Mom has been worried out of her mind about you and Chris. You really should have called her to let her know you'd had sense enough to get off the trail," Mac scolded.

Janey released a sigh. You'd think the goings-on at The Wedding Inn her mother owned and ran would be enough to keep anyone busy. "She's in the middle of a wedding, isn't she?"

"That doesn't stop her from worrying about all of us. You know that. She's been checking her machine every five minutes. And had she known what you were really up to tonight—" Mac frowned, recalling the kiss he had walked in on.

The kiss Janey would have given anything to have an instant replay of, before the passionate mood was spoiled, perhaps permanently. Not that she was looking for romance, she amended silently. Especially with a sports-minded man like Thad Lantz. On the other hand, there were principles to be adhered to. Ground rules to be set. And she had promised herself she would not allow any familial interference in her life when she left Colorado and moved back to North Carolina.

Janey wondered what it would take to show her family she was perfectly capable of living her life, and even embarking on new romance if she so chose, without their constant commentary and interference. She smiled at her brother sweetly, then warned, "One more word, Mac, and I swear I'm going to punch you out myself."

"I APOLOGIZE," Janey told Thad the moment Mac had left.

"Why?" Thad turned to face her, nothing but gentleness on his handsome face. "He obviously loves you a great deal. All your brothers do."

Janey shrugged, wishing Thad wasn't so understanding, so completely unruffled by the totally unnecessary family set-to he had just witnessed. It would make it easier for her to keep the emotional barriers up if he weren't so darn wonderful in all respects. She drew a bolstering breath. "That doesn't give them the right to interfere in my life," she countered stubbornly.

Thad took her hand in his and tugged her closer. "They're just reacting to any perceived dangers to you the same way you react to threats to Chris," he told her.

Janey hadn't really thought about it that way.

"I know," Thad continued understandingly, tightening his fingers on hers in a way she liked way too much, "because I have a younger sister, and I've been tempted to lock her up and throw away the key more times than I want to count."

Janey tried not to think how comforting it was to stand here, talking like this, even as she cautiously withdrew her hand from his lest it lead to anything else unsettlingly intimate—like more kisses. "Right. I know Molly," Janey said briskly, trying not to get too caught up in the moment and what had happened between them earlier. Like it or not, she still had a son to consider, a well-ordered life she didn't want turned on end. She'd had enough of that kind of uncertainty when she was married to Ty.

Ignoring the tingles in her hand, Janey continued. "She worked summers at The Wedding Inn before she went off to college. How old is she now?" she asked curiously, aware there was a pretty big age difference between Thad and Molly, as Molly was the child of his mother Veronica and Thad's stepfather, Lionel Lauder.

"Molly's twenty-one now and a college senior."

"At—?"

"Chapel Hill. And yes, she has a boyfriend, a pretty serious one at that."

Janey thought about what she had learned of local relationships, since she had moved back to town. "Johnny Byrne, isn't it?" He too had once bussed tables at The Wedding Inn and was now attending the University of North Carolina at Chapel Hill.

Thad nodded. "They've been dating for three years."

Janey didn't find that surprising—both were nice, well-rounded, clean-cut kids with the same strong work ethic and ambitious outlook on life. Yet she sensed a reservation in Thad akin to the one her brother Mac had just demonstrated. "Do you get along with Johnny?"

Thad fell silent, a conflicted expression on his face.

"You don't like him, do you?" Janey guessed.

Thad shrugged his powerful shoulders. "I'm just not sure he loves her the way he should. With all his heart and soul."

That was a surprisingly romantic thing for a guy to say.

"But, as you would no doubt point out," Thad continued with a resolve Janey couldn't help but respect, "Molly is a grown woman, so I'm just going to have to trust that she knows what she is doing."

"Mom!" Chris came out of the swinging double doors that fronted the terrace, as exuberant as ever. "There you are! Uncle Mac says we got to call Grandma."

"Yes," Janey said, realizing that Mac had sent Chris to make sure a repeat kiss would not happen, even if Chris didn't realize it. She smiled at her son. "We do."

Thad said a few kind words to Chris, then excused himself. To her disappointment, Janey did not see

Thad again before she and Chris checked out of the lodge the next morning. Because it was still raining, they had decided to go back to Holly Springs. She hoped Chris's nonstop chatter on the trip home about sports camp would help her get her mind off Thad Lantz and the way he had kissed her the night before.

THAD WAS HALFWAY HOME Sunday morning when he got the message from his mother, asking him to meet her in her office at noon over at the hospital's physical therapy department. "So what's the family crisis?" he asked when he got there, knowing immediately from the pinched, worried look on his normally un-flappable mother's face that something drastic had happened.

His mother looked up from the patient records she was going over. She gestured for Thad to have a seat, even as she pushed away from her desk. "Molly called from Gatlinburg. She and Johnny Byrne eloped."

Thad did a double take. "You're joking."

"Believe me," his mother replied ruefully as she ran a hand through her short and curly black hair, "I wish I was."

Thad stretched his long legs out in front of him. "Why would Molly do that?" Especially when Molly had been planning her nuptials—at least in theory—for years.

Veronica idly fingered the hospital ID badge clipped to her belt. "I have no idea."

"Is Lionel upset?"

Veronica made a beleaguered face. "What do you think?"

Given the fact that Molly was the apple of his step-father's eye, Thad thought, Lionel had to be furious, as well as hurt, at being shut out of this very important moment of his only daughter's life.

Veronica removed her glasses and rubbed the bridge of her nose. "I want you to talk to her when she gets back tomorrow, Thad. Try and see if you can figure out why she and Johnny went and did this."

Thad was glad to help in any way he could. "I'll try. She may not confide in me, though," he warned.

"Try anyway. And in the meantime, I'm going to pull together the best reception I can manage for the two of them. I just hope Delectable Cakes can do a wedding cake for them on such short notice."

Thad grinned as he thought about the pretty baker. "I can handle that for you, Mom," he said, glad for the excuse to go and see Janey again. "When do you want it?"

"Friday. It's the only evening I can get The Wedding Inn this week for a reception. And I only got that because of a cancellation." Veronica lifted a brow. "I wasn't aware you and Janey were friends."

"Her son is interested in attending the Storm's summer hockey camp," Thad replied casually.

"So are at least six hundred other boys." Veronica put her glasses back on. "I don't hear you talking about any of *their* mothers."

Touché. Briefly, Thad explained about the heart-rending letter he'd received from Chris.

Veronica's expression softened compassionately as she listened. "And something about Chris's plea really got to you," she noted finally.

Thad nodded. "I know how much it meant to me when Lionel helped me find the proper outlet for my own athletic ambitions." Thad loved his real father, but Gordon Lantz had never really understood Thad's desire to become involved in professional sports. Gordon had wanted Thad to become involved with the garden and landscape business that his own father had begun. It was his stepfather, Lionel, who had come into Thad's life when he was ten, and helped him find his way, in that regard. It was also how they'd became close.

"I can understand how you would want to do for someone else what Lionel did for you," Veronica stated gently. "And I know firsthand what a personable and winning kid Christopher Campbell is. I met him one day when he was out with his grandmother."

"But?" Thad prodded, hearing the concern underlying her words.

Veronica got up and removed two bottles of orange juice from her minifridge. She tossed one to him. "You're facing two major pitfalls here. The first is that anything you say or do on the subject has the potential to further the rift between Janey and her son Chris. And unless you want to make a sworn enemy of Janey, you need to make sure that doesn't happen. Because her relationship with her son is everything to her."

Thad hadn't needed to be told that. In Janey's

place, he would have felt the same. But he let his mother have her say, anyway. "And the second?"

"Issue concerns your own heart and happiness," Veronica continued with the practical plainspokenness she was known for both inside and outside the hospital. She paused, measuring her words carefully. "I know how much you enjoyed being a father when you were married to Renee, and that there's a hole in your life you've never really been able to fill since you lost your own stepson. According to his grandmother, Helen Hart, Christopher is reeling, too, from the loss of his dad."

So maybe it was destined, Thad thought, that he and Chris meet.

His mother, unfortunately, did not see it that way. She looked him straight in the eye and continued, "I would hate to see you use Chris—even subconsciously—to assuage that loss, Thad."

As if he would ever put the needs of any kid second to his own. "So you'd rather see me what?" Thad shot back angrily, setting the orange juice down unopened. "Walk away from a kid who looks up to me so much he asked for my help?" Thad had already abandoned one child—albeit reluctantly. It wasn't an experience he was looking to repeat. With anyone.

"I'm saying, honey, that I don't want you to make the same mistake twice. And from what I've heard, Janey had a rough enough time in her first marriage. Even if she won't quite admit it."

Thad got to his feet. He squared off with his mother

over her desk. ''I have no intention of hurting her,''
he said evenly. Or Christopher.

Veronica removed the plastic wrap from the top of
her bottle and tossed it in the waste can. ''You had
no intention of hurting Renee and Bobby, either. And
look what happened.''

THAD LEFT, furious with his mother.

He knew she was trying to help, but she had completely misunderstood the situation. Yes, he was
drawn to Janey's son, Christopher. Who wouldn't be?
The kid was remarkably bright, energetic, ready to
tackle life with so much gusto. Thad couldn't walk
away from the raw hope and need for understanding
he had seen shining in the boy's eyes. Chris had
reached out to him and Thad was honor bound to help
him. It was that simple.

As for Janey, well, Thad was mysteriously drawn
to her, too. He had known that the first second she
crashed into him, in the alley behind her bakery.

And that fascination had been confirmed every second since. It didn't matter whether they were talking,
sparring, or just looking at each other. When he was
with her, he was more completely in the moment than
he could ever recall being. And she felt it, too. He
saw it in her eyes, and he sure as heck had felt it in
her kiss.

Which gave him every reason in the world to pursue her.

And lucky him, he even had a rock-solid reason to

search her out immediately. And spend even more time with her.

Sunday afternoon, the Delectable Cakes bakery was closed.

Janey's minivan was parked in the driveway of her home. A magnificent white Bentley was idling at the curb. Hannah Reid, chief mechanic of Classic Car Auto Repair, and part-time chauffeur was seated behind the wheel. She was dressed in the usual man's tuxedo, cap tucked jauntily over her wavy auburn hair. Wondering what was up, Thad parked on the street behind the limo and walked up to say hello. Hannah put down her window. "Hey, Thad."

"Hey, Hannah."

"Do me a favor?" Hannah persuaded with a smile.

"Sure."

"Go around back and see if you can't get Dylan Hart to get his sorry self back in the limo. He's going to miss his flight to Chicago if we don't get a move on."

"No problem."

Thad headed around the side of Janey's small cottage-style home in the older section of Holly Springs. He had nearly rounded the corner of the one-and-a-half-story home when he heard the voices.

"Listen to me, Janey. Joe has had a rough enough start with the Storm, given what happened between him and the owner's daughter, without you luring Joe's coach out of town and kissing him like there's no tomorrow!"

"First of all, Joe and Emma are happily married

now. Joe's conflict with Saul Donovan is a thing of the past. And second, I did not lure Thaddeus Lantz anywhere!'' Janey protested heatedly as an interested Thad stopped where he was.

''Then how do you explain Thad following you out to Lake Pine?'' Dylan asked.

That was just it, Thad thought. They couldn't. Because to tell the truth, it was quite unlike him. Usually, he didn't give the women around him—even those he was wildly physically attracted to—a second thought. These days, his thoughts were all on the team he was coaching, and his desire to make it to the Stanley Cup finals. Not sometime in the very far future. But this very year. With the very team he was going to be coaching through training camp, come the second week of September.

Usually, this time of year, he was focused on the upcoming season, and figuring out how to make sure each and every player on the Storm roster reached his full potential. Instead, he was, more often than not, thinking about Janey Hart Campbell and her son.

''For Joe's sake,'' Dylan continued firmly, in much the same vein as his brother Mac. ''You have to stay away from Thaddeus Lantz! I mean it, Janey. No more kissing Joe's coach!''

Thad rounded the corner. He looked from Janey to Dylan, and back again, before asking lazily. ''Bad time?''

''Actually,'' Janey said sweetly, her temper obviously getting the best of her at long last, ''It's the perfect time.'' Her chin set determinedly, she marched past Dylan, wrapped her arms around Thad's shoulders, went up on tiptoe and planted one on him.

Her lips were every bit as soft and sweet and warm as he recalled. Pleasure zinged through him as he wrapped both his arms around her, as casually as if they did this every day. Following her lead, he kissed her right back, every bit as thoroughly as he had the evening before, until he felt her melting against him. And then, only then, did he let the heated caress come to a lazy halt and lift his head ever so slowly from hers.

Janey looked up into his face, a mixture of shock and passion reflected in her soft amber eyes. Clearly, she had wanted him to play along with her, to pretend this was some grand passion to simultaneously egg her brother on and punish him for getting involved in her business. She hadn't wanted Thad to get so carried away… But that, Thad thought, was just what happened when they kissed, even when it was all for show.

"Okay," Dylan grumbled from the left of them. He glared at Thad, then Janey. "You've more than made your point, sis. You can kiss whomever you want. And it appears Thad here can take care of himself."

"You're right about that," Thad said. Even if he didn't quite like the way he had just been used to make a point, one Hart sibling to another.

Janey wiped imaginary specks of dirt from what Thad guessed were her gardening clothes—a pair of old cutoff jeans with frayed edges, and a T-shirt that was a little too snug across the breasts for his comfort. Dylan, on the other hand, was clad in a sharp suit and tie befitting an up-and-coming TV sportscaster. "Your limo is waiting," Thad told Dylan, recalling why he had come around the side of the house in the first place. "Hannah Reid said to get a move on or you're going to miss your flight."

"We shouldn't have dragged you into the situation with Chris," Dylan stated with frank apology.

"You didn't. Chris did. And I don't mind," Thad said quietly, in the same man-to-man tone. He liked helping the boy. Liked feeling needed. "What I do mind—" Thad clapped his hand on Dylan's shoulder, the same way he did when he was coaching one of his players in a tense situation "—is you interfering in my romantic life or lack thereof." Thad looked him straight in the eye, making sure he had Dylan's full attention before he continued. "Got it?"

Dylan's jaw tightened. The look in his eyes was mutinous.

"It was unfortunate your brother Mac walked in on what he did last night, out at Lake Pine. It doesn't make it any of his business. Or yours. Janey and I are adults. We will figure this out without any help from either of our families." And that included his mother, Thad thought. Well-meaning or not, she was going to have to stay out of this.

Embarrassment staining his handsome face, Dylan nodded his understanding reluctantly. Then he looked Thad straight in the eye. "Joe's boss or not—you do anything to hurt her and you'll have the whole Hart posse coming after you.''

Thad dropped his hand from Dylan's shoulder. Winning Janey's heart would first require running the gauntlet of Hart men. Thad knew he was more than up to the task. ''I'd expect nothing less,'' he said. In fact, it was reassuring to him, knowing Janey's family loved her that much.

With a careless nod in both their directions, Dylan took off.

Flushing more than Dylan had been, Janey propped the backs of her gloved hands on her waist. Shaking her head, as if unable to believe his penchant for arriving at the most inopportune times, she stepped away from Thad. ''Sorry about that. Again,'' she said heatedly.

Thad grinned, loving the way she looked, all disheveled and flushed and perspiring. Which was probably the way she would one day look in his bed, in the throes of passion.

''I'm not,'' Thad said, moving closer.

Janey shook her head in silent self-admonition and refused to meet his gaze. ''I probably shouldn't have kissed you,'' she murmured in a low, throaty tone.

''Probably not, if it was for all the wrong reasons. Then again, if it's for all the right reasons, like this…'' he wrapped his arms around her and kissed her sweetly, tenderly, until she trembled in his arms once again, ''I don't mind at all.''

A guilty flush stained her cheeks. She lowered her glance. Refusing to acknowledge their latest kiss, or her potent reaction to it, she splayed her hands across his chest and murmured, "What I was trying to say Thad, is that there seems to be no shortage of embarrassing family moments on my behalf for you to witness."

Trying not to feel disappointed she had used their mutual attraction to make a point with her family, Thad shrugged. And because it was what she seemed to want, he let her go. "They just don't want to see you hurt. I can understand that. As I said, I am equally as protective about my sister. Which, by the way, is why I'm here. Molly has eloped."

Janey blinked, her full attention on him once again. "With Johnny Byrne?"

"Yesterday, apparently."

"Why?"

"That's just it. Nobody knows. They're still in Gatlinburg. Due back tomorrow. Anyway, my mother and stepfather want to put together a reception for the two of them. Friday is the only evening this week The Wedding Inn is open. My mother is hoping you're not too busy to make the cake."

She shot him an unexpectedly flirtatious glance. "Ah. And you're here to persuade me." She seemed to like the idea.

An answering warmth sizzled through him. "I volunteered."

As she tilted her head to the side, the silky chestnut strands that had escaped her hair clip gently brushed the slender nape of her neck. "Well, I do owe you a favor." Her eyes twinkled merrily.

"Which is the polite way of saying you're already booked."

Janey stepped closer and stood, gloved hands on her hips, legs braced apart, her sneaker-clad feet planted firmly in the grass that edged her vegetable garden. "I can fit it in." She paused to wet her lips. "I'm going to have to know what kind of cake they want, though."

"I'll have Molly and Johnny come over to your shop tomorrow, as soon as they arrive," Thad promised, thinking he might stop by, too. After all, he was on his own schedule, this time of year. It wouldn't be that way two months from now. Which meant whatever courting had to be done to make her his, would have to be done now. And he did want to make her his. "So what are you doing here?" He nodded at the garden.

"Weeding. Or trying to—I don't seem to be getting very far." She dropped to her knees beside the row of bush beans, and picked up her hand tool. "Want to help?"

Thad made a face as he hunkered down beside her. He knew it wasn't going to win him any points with her, but he decided to be honest with her anyway. "It's not really my thing."

She shot him a glance from beneath a fringe of thick, chestnut-colored lashes. "That's surprising, given the fact your dad owns a gardening and landscape business."

Deciding if he was going to hang around, he might as well get comfortable, Thad shrugged and dropped to the grass beside her. He reclined next to her, long legs stretched out, the weight of his torso resting on his bent elbow. ''I never was much for rooting around in the dirt.''

She rooted out a sticker bush and a clump of dandelion with a practiced motion of the spade and set them aside. ''Nicely put.''

''Not that you don't look good doing it.'' She did. She really did. Watching the play of worn denim across her slender thighs and delectably sweet butt, and the taut stretch of cotton across her breasts, it was all he could do not to tumble her here and now and see how far he'd get in his pursuit of her. The responsible adult part of her might protest, but the reckless impetuous woman and wild heart inside would probably be all for it.

Unfortunately, the fact was they were in broad daylight, and there wasn't so much as a privacy fence or decent hedge to shield them from the prying eyes of the neighbors, so any real move on his part would have to wait.

She grinned over at him. ''Flattery will get you precisely...nowhere.''

''Then how about a date?'' Thad asked, beginning to realize he wanted a lot more than a few stolen kisses or casual conversations with her. He let his glance rove her hair, her face, her lips, before returning ever so slowly and deliberately to her molten amber eyes. ''Where will that get me?''

Chapter Four

"You've got to be kidding," Janey said, wishing she had on something aside from her threadbare shorts and T-shirt.

Thad continued reclining beside her, looking like there was no place on earth he would rather be. "Do I look like I'm kidding?" he asked with a sexy half smile.

No, Janey thought. He looked like he wanted to kiss her again. And she couldn't allow that. Not when she had inadvertently given so much of her feelings away, so quickly already. Hadn't she learned her lesson when she had gotten involved so quickly with Ty? Hadn't the years of marital misery taught her anything about the dangers of investing her heart in what was, at best, a short-lived passion?

Yes, Thad was by far the best kisser she had ever met. And was probably the best lover, as well, although she promised herself she would never find that out. But she couldn't—wouldn't—let herself sink back into the cycle of recklessness and regret that had so characterized her early life. She was an adult now, a mother of a twelve-year-old boy. She had a duty to herself and to Chris to behave responsibly. And responsible mothers did not indulge in exciting, passionate love affairs that burned white-hot, for an exhilarating time, and then faded, leaving the ex-lovers feeling drained and disillusioned, emptier than before.

But not about to get into all that with Thad, she only said, "I thought we agreed that my son is going to be working for you, picking up towels in the locker room or something." She just hadn't told Chris yet.

"Not me, per se," Thad corrected. "The team. And this date isn't for you and Chris and me. It's for you and me."

Precisely what she was afraid of. Because thus far she hadn't been able to be alone with Thad for fifteen minutes without kissing him. There was no telling what would happen on a five- or six-hour date, where they were likely to be quite alone, at least for part of the evening. "I can't." She didn't want to risk him putting the moves on her, and her saying yes, yes, yes.

Thad frowned and sat up, cross-legged, in the grass. "Because of what your brother said? Because I have to tell you—me seeing you socially won't affect how I treat your brother Joe in the slightest."

Janey had only to look at Thad's face to confirm work was work for Thad, his feelings for her something else indeed. She blushed self-consciously despite herself. "I know that."

He plucked a few blades of grass, rubbed them sensually between his fingertips, watching her all the while. "Then—?"

Janey turned her glance back to his face. Needing something to concentrate on other than the steadily building emotional and physical attraction between them, she noticed that although he had showered and washed his hair that morning, he hadn't shaved. "I just don't think it's a good idea."

"To date me or to date anyone?" Thad asked.

Trying hard not to notice how alluring and faintly dangerous the day's worth of stubble made him look, Janey took in a steadying breath and plastered her most devil-may-care expression on her face. "To date anyone."

His eyes darkened sympathetically. "Why not?"

Janey shrugged. She really didn't want to get into this with him. Didn't want him tearing down her arguments one by one. Insinuating himself in her mind and her heart, until all she could think about, wish for, was even more time with him than she had already had. "I've got a pretty full life as it is, with my business and my son. I don't want to complicate things," she stated simply.

Thad shrugged his powerful shoulders and rose gracefully to his feet. He dusted the grass off his jeans. "Fair enough."

Janey tried—and then failed—not to be disappointed he backed off so readily as she remained in the grass, kneeling next to her vegetable garden.

"All right. I'll see you tomorrow at the shop, then," Thad promised.

Just when you thought it was safe to go back in the water, Janey thought. "For what?" she asked, aware her heart was pounding and she was tingling all over.

Thad smiled down at her as he hooked his thumbs through the loops on either side of his fly and rocked back on his heels. "I'll be coming by with my sister, Molly, and her new husband."

Deciding suddenly it wasn't a good idea for her to be doing something that put her at eye level with the most masculine part of his anatomy, Janey stood and dusted off her knees. Pretending to be impervious to his sexy presence, she asked curiously, "Molly needs you to help pick out the cake?"

He grinned mischievously, and sidestepping the question, said with a teasing wink, "I hear free samples are involved."

Who would have thought a man as physically fit as Thad would have a weakness for something made of sugar and butter and eggs? "And you like cake," she guessed.

"Oh yeah. And then some," he said, making it sound somehow sexual. Whistling, he thrust his hands in his pockets and sauntered off, as cheerfully as if she had accepted his invitation to go out with him, after all.

BUT AS IT TURNED OUT, Thad did not walk in with Johnny Byrne and Molly the next afternoon. Nor did they make any mention of Molly's older half brother as they quickly got down to business with Janey.

"Look, I know my parents are trying to go all out with this party at The Wedding Inn, but it doesn't have to be an actual wedding cake. It could just be a sheet cake," Molly said, looking impossibly young in a college T-shirt, shorts, and flip-flops. Like her brother Thad, the pretty young bride had dark curly hair and electric blue eyes, and a lithe, naturally athletic form.

Johnny, who was also clad in a T-shirt, shorts and sneakers, nodded, too. "A regular cake is fine with me," he said. Though his manner was polite, he looked as if he would rather be anywhere else doing anything else. Not the attitude Janey would have expected. Even though her own marriage had been all wrong, the days following her own elopement had been heady with passion and excitement. She had been so certain, initially, everything was going to work out great. These two kids looked almost depressed. As well as so very young, Janey thought. She continued to study the couple before her, trying to figure out what might make them happy, cakewise, while pleasing the parents involved, too. "I don't think that's what your mother had in mind, Molly," Janey said gently. She had spoken to Veronica on the phone that morning. Veronica wanted to go all out.

Molly rolled her eyes in exasperation. "Johnny and I are already married. There's no reason for us to be having a reception at all," Molly said. Beside her, Johnny seemed to agree.

The bell over the door rang as Thad walked into the shop. Janey did her best to ignore the leap her heart took at the sight of him. And her joy had little to do with the difficult situation he could help her smooth over. She just liked seeing him, being with him.

''I think our mother would beg to differ with you,'' Thad told Molly. ''So would Lionel, for that matter.''

Molly turned rebellious eyes to Thad. She looked more surly teen now than blushing bride. ''What are you doing here?''

''Mom asked me to stop by. Make sure it all went smoothly. She would have been here herself, but she was booked solid over at the physical therapy department today.''

''Well, that's a relief,'' Molly said, sighing.

Johnny turned to Molly. ''Mind if I get going now?'' he asked.

Molly shook her head. She looked as if she wanted to get rid of him. ''Go ahead,'' she said.

Johnny mumbled a goodbye and rushed out the door, head down. Molly looked relieved to see her new husband go. Thad studied Molly, with lifted brow. Janey had an idea what Thad was feeling. Something was wrong here. Molly's behavior didn't make sense. And neither did Johnny's. They should be deliriously happy, in full newlywed mode, whether they had eloped in private or walked down a church aisle, in front of all their family and friends. Molly and Johnny shouldn't want to be separated for even a moment, and when they were together, they shouldn't be able to keep their hands off each other.

Instead, they had looked anything but madly, passionately in love.

"I can talk to your mother," Janey offered. "Tell her you would prefer something much simpler than the traditional seven-layer wedding cake she had in mind."

Molly waved off Janey's offer desultorily. "Mom's not going to agree," Molly predicted glumly. "She said Johnny and I deprived her and Daddy of the wedding. She's not going to let us rob them of the reception, too. So you two pick it out. Just whatever you think she wants is fine with the two of us. Now, I've gotta go."

"Where can I reach you?" Thad asked, following her to the door. "Your campus apartment or Johnny's?"

Molly's cheeks turned bright pink as she stared down at the car keys in her hand. "Actually, we're not going to live together just yet," Molly said. "Our apartment leases aren't up for another six weeks. So we've got till then to convince our roommates to move out and give us the apartment or find another place." She rushed out the door before Thad could ask anything else.

An awkward silence fell. Thad turned back to Janey, looking frustrated and concerned as well as mystified. "What do you want to do about the cake?" Janey asked him.

Thad shrugged, his previously mentioned interest in tasting samples all but gone. "Just go with whatever is most traditional."

"That would be a three-tiered white cake with vanilla butter-cream frosting, and probably some flowers
on it, maybe a bride and groom on top of it."

"Sounds great."

Janey wrote up the order, and handed him the customer copy.

Thad lingered, in no more hurry to leave than she
was to see him go. "You eloped, too, didn't you? I
was in my senior year at Clarkson University then—
but I remember hearing something about it at the
time. It was pretty big news around here."

Janey nodded wryly, recalling the brouhaha. "I
shocked everyone. Went out to Colorado on spring
break to ski with a bunch of my friends, and met Ty.
And five days later, we eloped. I called my mom from
Colorado. Needless to say, she was *not* happy."

"Did you have 'eloper's remorse'—like Molly and
Johnny?"

Janey cut them both a slice of one of her sample
cakes—white genoise sponge cake soaked in black-
currant liqueur and frosted with marzipan icing. "Not
for a while. But it was all so new to me. I was only
nineteen at the time, and I'd never been seriously involved with anyone. It was all very passionate and
exciting until I got pregnant with Christopher." She
gestured Thad to come to the rear of the bakery,
where she baked the sugary confections.

"And then?" Thad asked, as Janey lifted two
wooden stools over to the butcher-block worktable in
the center of the kitchen.

"Then reality hit," Janey confessed as she sat

down, kitty-corner from him, and they both forked up some cake. "It was no longer fun to be living in a dive, or struggling to make ends meet while Ty worked odd jobs at ski resorts and trained for the U.S.A. tryouts for the Olympics."

Thad searched her eyes. "But you loved him."

I loved who I thought he was.

Janey was silent, not sure what to say, without feeling disloyal, or betraying the vows she had once taken. Marriage was a sacred trust. Or it should have been. "In retrospect, I think I was confused by the physical side of things in our relationship. I mistook passion for love. By the time I realized Ty and I weren't really suited, we had Christopher. We both loved him, and wanted what was best for him, regardless of the flaws in our relationship, Ty was a good father to Chris. He really loved him, and Chris loved his dad. I couldn't separate the two, especially when I knew what it was like to grow up without a dad."

Thad's gaze gentled compassionately as she got up to pour them both some coffee. "How old were you when your dad died?" he asked.

"Almost thirteen." Their hands brushed as she handed him a steaming mug. "How old were you when your parents got divorced?"

"Two. So I didn't remember it at all. I was lucky though. Mom and Dad were able to be amicable with each other. When Mom married Lionel, it was like I had two dads. So I didn't suffer in that regard."

"I'm glad," Janey said.

It was important to have your parents' love, even if they didn't always quite "get" you.

"But back to Molly," Thad continued easily enough. Finished with his cake, he pushed the plate away. "Do you have any idea what might be causing her to react this way?"

One, Janey thought. But she didn't want to mention it.

Thad looked her in the eye. Once again, he seemed able to read her mind. "You're thinking what I'm thinking, aren't you?" he guessed softly, after a moment.

Janey paused, her mug halfway to her lips. "Which is?"

"That she might be pregnant?"

FOR A SECOND, Janey didn't say anything. She just continued to look at him, and Thad gazed back, enjoying the experience of sitting there with her, talking with the familiar intimacy of two people who had known each other for years instead of just a few days. It was funny. He felt he knew everything about her, and at the same time, there was so much more he wanted to learn about her. And vowed he would.

"It would certainly explain Molly's ambivalence and the rush to tie the knot," Janey remarked finally.

Molly and Johnny had been dating now for three years, Thad thought, and getting pretty close in the process. At least from what he could see.

"Can you ask her about it?" Janey asked, her eyes softening compassionately.

Thad wished it were that easy. He shook his head. "There's a fifteen-year age difference between us. By the time she was three, I was off to college, then working my first job as assistant coach in the minors. We love each other, but we're not able to talk...not like that." Much to his regret.

Janey seemed to understand. She ran her fingers absently across the smooth stoneware surface of her mug. "Actually, she might not be able to come to you with something like that even if you were closer in age, you being a guy and all. She might feel more comfortable talking to one of her female friends."

Aware her idle actions were reminding him of other, more intimate things, Thad moved his eyes away from the gentle, stroking ministrations of her soft, feminine hands. "You think she has?"

Janey hesitated. "I think if she hasn't done so yet she will soon. Maybe she'll even go to your mom. Right now, she seems to have a lot on her plate, with the reception your mother and stepfather want to give her on Friday."

"That's true," Thad said, as the bell above the door rang out in the silence of the shop. Chris came bursting through the door on his skateboard, backpack slung over one shoulder. He slid straight through the round tables of display cakes, past the counter, into the kitchen where the two of them sat. If he had any objection about the way they were sitting there chatting, not to mention the mutual interest and chemistry he and Janey were finding it more and more difficult to hide, Christopher did not show it.

Janey lifted a censuring brow.

Before she could get a word in, Chris had tipped the skateboard up on one end and tucked it beneath his arm, out of harm's way of the cakes in progress. "Hey, Mom. Coach Lantz," he greeted them both cheerfully.

"Hello, Christopher." Thad put out his hand, and the two of them slapped palms.

"Did you talk to your teacher about camp?" Janey asked.

Chris nodded. He set his backpack and skateboard down in the corner, then went straight to the refrigerator and emerged with an individual carton of milk and a handful of the chocolate chip cookies she kept just for him. "She said I can go. She'll get me an excused absence from the summer school principal. All I gotta do is get next week's work done in advance," Chris continued between mouthfuls of cookie and long thirsty gulps of milk. "She gave me all the assignments this afternoon. I can turn them in on Friday."

Janey seemed pleased. "I'll help you after work."

"Uh...thanks, Mom, but—" Chris slanted a look at Thad, before turning back to Janey, "I, uh, I don't think that's such a good idea. You know what happened the last time you helped me with integers," Chris continued while Janey flushed a telltale pink. "I flunked the assignment. And this next section is all about well—never mind." Chris waved his hand back and forth, as if erasing a blackboard. "There's no sense in me trying to explain. 'Cause you won't get it anyway. But that's okay.'' Chris grinned at his mom affectionately. ''Uncle Mac and Uncle Fletch said they'd help me when they get off work at five. I'm meeting them at Downtown Pizza, if that's okay with you.''

''As long as you're going to be there,'' Janey said, going to her purse, ''bring us home a pepperoni pizza when you're through.''

''THAD—I MEAN Coach Lantz—really knows his stuff,'' Chris told Janey that evening as he simultaneously set a pizza box on the kitchen table and dropped his book bag on the floor. ''Even Uncle Mac and Uncle Fletcher were impressed.''

Janey got two plates down from the cupboard. Chris held up his hand. ''I don't want any. I already ate with the guys. Well...'' He had second thoughts as Janey lifted the lid and the delicious smell of pepperoni and green-pepper pizza wafted into the room. ''Maybe just two pieces.''

Janey poured Chris some milk, some spring water for herself, and sat down opposite him. ''I don't understand how Thad ended up helping you with your math tonight.''

''He came into Downtown Pizza. And while he was waiting on his take-out order he came over to talk to us, and realized my uncles were explaining it all wrong. So he helped me out. He also told me how important math is for hockey players.''

''He did, did he?''

Chris nodded soberly. "I gotta pay a lot more attention to what's going on."

So did Janey. For completely different reasons.

Bad enough that she was wildly attracted to Thad Lantz. So much so that she still couldn't forget the sweet, scintillating intensity of his kisses. Without Chris going ga-ga over him, too.

She knew Chris missed his dad.

That he was looking to fill the hole in his life left with Ty's death. His uncles had all tried to be there for him, but Chris wanted a real dad again. And Janey had the sinking feeling she knew exactly who he had picked out for that position.

THAD HAD JUST SETTLED down with the latest copy of *The Sporting News* when he heard a loud pounding on the front door. Wondering who was making that kind of racket, he put down his magazine and headed for the foyer. A sheepish-looking Janey Hart Campbell was standing on the stoop. She looked different somehow. Maybe because of the way she had dressed, in a turquoise summer sweater set and stone-colored above-the-knee skirt and sandals. It was a very pulled-together look, the kind of thing she'd wear to a PTA meeting. Her hair, too, was different. Usually, she wore the heavy length of it up in a clip. Tonight, it was flowing in tousled waves over her shoulders. It looked so soft and touchable he longed to run his fingers through it. But knew if he did that he'd just end up kissing her again. Kissing her and not wanting to stop...

"Sorry for banging so loud but your doorbell seems to be broken," she began in a bright, overly cheerful tone.

"I keep meaning to have it fixed," Thad explained, his eyes still fixed on her face. Damn, but she looked pretty—even at nine o'clock at night on a Monday evening. And she smelled fantastic, too. Like expensive perfume.

"I wanted to drop this off for Chris." She handed him the camp application and a personal check.

His heartbeat sped up as their hands touched. "It could have waited until morning."

"I know, but what I have to say to you *can't* wait." Janey glanced cautiously behind her at the row of exclusive new half-million-dollar homes, so unlike her own neighborhood of small, homey abodes.

Was that why she had dressed up? Thad wondered. Because she had driven over to his part of town?

Or was there some other, more subtle, more important message she was trying to impart to him?

"Mind if I come in for a few minutes?" she asked.

Mind? Hell, it was what he had wanted in the first place, as he recalled, though he couldn't exactly deem this a date. "Be my guest."

He ushered her inside, but when he attempted to show her into the living room where he had been sitting, relaxing, she dug in her heels. "Really, this is fine."

Obviously, she wasn't staying. Thad put the camp application and check down on the hall table beside his keys, so he wouldn't forget it when he left the next morning. Then he did his best to disguise his disappointment as he waited for her to say what she had to say.

"Chris told me you helped him with his math this evening."

Guilt flooded him. Ah, hell. Was that what this was about? She didn't trust the bond growing between him and her son, either? Thad nodded, showing his best poker face. "Bright kid. He catches on fast."

"He's also very enamored of you."

Thad had noticed—it was a reaction he got from a lot of twelve-year-old boys who were interested in hockey. But Janey wasn't happy about it. Maybe because she feared what would happen if Thad took her son into his heart or become a father figure to him. But that *wasn't* what was happening here, Thad thought. He was a friend to Chris, a role model. Nothing more. And Janey needed to know that. "I wouldn't worry about his mild case of hero worship. It's likely to fade quickly as soon as he gets to know me," Thad teased.

The amusement he had hoped to see in her eyes was nowhere to be found. "In any case, I don't want him going to you that way," Janey continued soberly.

Now it was Thad's turn to take offense at what was going on between the three of them. "He didn't come to me for help," Thad explained. "I approached him."

"You know what I mean," Janey said, her hands twisting into fists.

"Yeah, I think I do," Thad agreed, stepping closer.

"And your pique has nothing to do with my tutoring your son."

Janey's mouth dropped open.

"It has to do with me," Thad asserted confidently, knowing finally why she had really come over there to see him, with all her emotional armor on. "And the fact I kissed you and you kissed me back."

JANEY HAD KNOWN it was a mistake to come over, but she hadn't been able to help herself then, any more than she could keep herself from putting up the emotional defenses that had served her so well in the past. Thad lifted a goading brow, waiting it seemed, for her to make that first verbal mistake. "You're putting too much on a kiss," she stated archly. *And so for that matter was she.*

Thad grinned at her. "Or two or three or four."

He was looking at her as if he wanted nothing more than to make love to her then and there, Janey noticed. She hitched in a breath as her pulse jumped and skittered and tried again to get the upper hand in this conversation. She regarded him sternly. "A kiss is just a kiss."

"Ah. There are kisses," he said, taking her abruptly into his arms, and pressing her close, so they were touching in one long electric line. "And then," he said, even more softly, as the seductive smile curving his lips spread to his eyes, "there are kisses. And what we have, Janey Hart, are kisses."

Ignoring her soft gasp of surprise, he delivered a long, breath-stealing kiss that quickly had her middle fluttering weightlessly and her nipples aching. Feelings swept through her, passionate, intense and true.

She surged against him, and he kissed her again and again and again, so thoroughly that her knees went weak and she moaned low in her throat, despite herself.

It felt so good to be held and touched and kissed like this. So good to be wanted. To have the barriers between them start coming down. She melted against him, need pouring through her. She felt his arousal pressing against her, hot and urgent, his heart pounding against her chest, every bit as strong and erratically as hers. And she knew if she did give in to the yearning inundating her heart and soul and make love with him she would never be the same again. Never see him or herself in the same way. Panicking a little at the fierceness of her emotions, she pushed him away, drew in a shuddering breath. "Please, Thad—"

He held her eyes with his mesmerizing ocean-blue gaze, making her feel even more hot and bothered inside. "Please what?"

She turned her gaze away from his brawny chest and powerful shoulders. "Please don't hurt my son." *Or me,* she thought, well aware she did not have to give in to his easy southern charm or boundless determination. Just because he was more inherently sexy and deeply chivalrous than anyone she had ever met did not mean they were meant to have their lives entwined in even deeper and more meaningful ways. It didn't mean she had to keep fantasizing about what it might be like to actually make love with him.

She hitched in a tremulous breath and forced her eyes to his. "Because I don't think I could bear it. You have no idea how much he adores you and looks up to you, and if Chris were to get even the slightest wind of this flirtation that's been going on between us, he'd jump to all sorts of conclusions."

Just like I'm starting to jump to conclusions. Like the one that has you falling for me every bit as hard and irrevocably as I am starting to fall for you.

Thad lifted a curious brow. "You think he'd figure we were sleeping together?"

Shock permeated her brain. "Of course not! He's knows I'm not that kind of woman!" *Even if you make me feel like that kind of woman.*

He regarded her with an unrepentant half smile and goaded gently, "The kind who has a love life?"

Janey flushed. "The kind who sleeps around!" she corrected with a haughty toss of her hair.

The humor left his eyes. "Trust me, Janey, no one would ever think that about you."

Doing her best to keep a level head, Janey stepped back a pace and folded her arms in front of her. Suddenly, she wished he didn't hold her in such high esteem. It would be so much easier to resent him if he saw her as an easy conquest. "Why do you say that?" she challenged quietly.

His expression turned all the more serious. "Because you don't put out that kind of vibe," he told her with so much gentleness that it nearly made her weep. "You're a hearts and flowers, have to be in love kind of woman. And I suspect your son knows that even if he's too young to be able to articulate it.''

His matter-of-fact words were reassuring to Janey. Still, she had come here for a reason, and she had to follow through on that. Had to make Thad see that it wasn't just their feelings involved here. "Chris is starting to want to see me married again.''

Finally, Thad looked a little surprised. "He said that?''

"He's been dropping hints.'' She pressed her lips together firmly. "He misses having a dad in the house with us.''

Finally, Thad seemed to be getting the reason behind her reticence to get romantically involved with him. His brow lifted. "And you think—?''

"I think he's very young. And impressionable. And he really worships you and you seem to sort of like him—''

"More than sort of like, Janey,'' Thad interrupted. "He's a great kid. A man would be lucky to call him son.''

"You see what I mean?'' she countered emotionally. "That just makes it worse!''

"How?'' Thad frowned in frustration.

Janey shrugged. "You really like Chris. Chris really likes you.''

The smile was back in his eyes, the come-on curve to his lips. "I really like you, too,'' he murmured.

Janey swallowed and moved away from him, pacing the length of the foyer. When he followed her a bit too closely, she walked into the masculinely appointed living room. She moved behind a dark tan wing chair and wrapped her hands over the back of it, struggling to remain strong. ''What happens if that interest fades?''

He edged closer, his lips taking on a sober line. ''And I lose interest in you?''

Janey held her ground with effort. ''Right.''

''Where does that leave you and Chris?'' he guessed, eyeing her with a depth of male speculation she found very disturbing.

''You can see how awkward it would be. I wouldn't want Chris to start to look to you for things, and you not want to be around me—and by association him—and he not understand why you walked away.''

Thad stood with his feet braced apart. He jammed his hands on his hips and narrowed his eyes. ''You've got this all figured out, don't you?'' he said, not seeming at all pleased by her conclusions.

''I've been—'' Hurt before, Janey almost said, but didn't.

Thad paused, looked her up and down from the top of her tousled chestnut hair to the tips of her toes, before returning his glance ever so slowly to hers. And she knew then he wasn't giving up or bowing out, not without a fight.

Chapter Five

"What was your relationship with your husband really like? You never said how Ty treated you during the years you were married."

"Why is it important?" she asked as she walked away from him, not stopping until she reached the other side of the living room.

Thad lounged against the back of the sofa, his hips resting on the top edge, his long legs stretched out in front of him. Continuing to scrutinize her with unremitting interest, he crossed his arms in front of him. "Because somehow what happened then is affecting what's happening with you and me now," Thad said quietly. "And I want to understand why you're so mistrustful of me and my motives. It can't be anything I've done."

Guilt wound its way into her heart. "You're right." She drew a stabilizing breath and tried to slow her racing pulse. She could tell by the way he was looking at her a lot was riding on her answer. "It's not."

"So?"

Telling him the truth meant breaking down the illusions that had so defined her life for so long. And yet for reasons she didn't completely understand, Janey found herself wanting to confide in him, even if it meant sacrificing her pride.

"You have to understand," she said softly, as she raked her teeth across her lower lip and plunged on, "I wanted our relationship to work. I tried to be a good wife."

"And—?" Thad's handsome face was tinged with compassion.

Janey shrugged, embarrassed by how miserable she had been then, how devastatingly alone. "He just... wasn't interested. Every day that passed, particularly after my body began to change with pregnancy and Chris was born, he adored me less and less until—I don't know—I guess we were more roommates and coparents than anything else."

Thad closed the distance between them with easy, sensual grace. He took her hand and held it tenderly. "You stayed because of Chris."

Janey nodded, her mood turning as grim as her life back then. She looked down at their clasped hands. His palm was so much larger and stronger. And yet her smaller, more delicate one fit into it perfectly.

"And my sense of responsibility," she continued ruefully, lifting her gaze back to mesh with his. "My mother and brothers had all disapproved of my foolish marriage from the start. I couldn't come back here and tell them they were all correct in their assumptions that Ty would not make me happy or love me the way I needed to be loved. No matter how much I regretted what I had done.''

There would have been way too many I-told-you-so's. Way too many lectures on the innate recklessness she was still battling to this day.

''And you did regret the marriage,'' Thad surmised seriously, tightening his fingers on hers.

''Yes.'' Janey took his other hand in hers, too, and rested her fingers snugly in his. ''Within two or three weeks, I realized I had mistaken passion for love. But by then it was too late. I was already pregnant. I had to think about the baby and what was best and that was a two-parent family.''

''In your situation I probably would have done the same,'' he told her candidly, understanding darkening his deep blue eyes. ''As for the rest...'' He paused. ''I think you're being way too hard on yourself. So you made a mistake in selecting a mate. So what? So did I the first time around.''

''What happened?''

''In a nutshell? Money meant more to her than me. The point is, Janey, one bad marriage doesn't mean you're consigned to spend the rest of your life celibate.''

How like a man to make a mistake, forget it, and move on without ever looking back. Whereas Janey couldn't do that. Recalling her errors in judgment and the havoc they had caused helped her to keep from repeating them all over again, and slipping back into the cycle of recklessness and regret that had marked her teenage years when she had been in an emotional tailspin after her father's death.

"Passion and fast action made a wreck of my life before, because I didn't understand that passion like that always fades and actions that aren't properly thought out and examined beforehand often have dire consequences."

"Passion does not always fade," he countered, looking impossibly handsome and determined in the soft light. "And fast actions are usually the best ones, because they come from your gut before you have a chance to think something to death and somehow muck it up."

Janey shook her head, exasperated. "Spoken like a true coach."

He winked at her confidently. "I'll take that as a compliment."

"I was sure you would," Janey retorted drolly, not sure she liked that bold, rapacious gleam in his eyes.

"And—" Using his grip on her hand, he hauled her against him, then shifted positions, so her back was to the wall, her front blanketed by the steely warmth of his tall frame. "I'll prove both theories to you the best way I know how," he promised softly, as her body pulsed with need.

The next thing Janey knew he was cupping her face in his hands, angling his head to allow better access to hers. She barely had time to gasp, whether in indignation or excitement she couldn't say, and then they were kissing in a way that felt incredibly right. Her excitement mounted as he sucked at her bottom lip and touched the tip of her tongue with his while he moved his hands up and down her spine. Their breathing grew louder and more unsteady, even as the core of her didn't want to give in to him, didn't want to surrender her heart and soul to him. Yet as he continued to kiss her deliberately, rubbing his lips across hers, stroking the insides of her mouth with his tongue again and again she found herself surging closer and wrapping her arms around him.

Pressing her slender body against the warm, muscular length of his, she kissed him back hotly, wantonly. His hands slid around to find her breasts, cupping gently as his kiss deepened, bringing forth responses she didn't know she had in her. Torrid feelings she wanted to feel again and again and again. Had she ever wanted this completely or desperately? Had anyone ever made her feel this womanly and sensual and free? Janey only knew she wanted him to kiss her and caress her and yes—even make love to her—if that would make all the hurt from her past, all the despair and the loneliness and the worry over her future go away.

Thad hadn't intended to make Janey his when he'd hauled her into his arms. All he had wanted to do was show her that she still had a lot more life and love left in her than she thought, that she'd be a fool to throw away her future—not to mention the chemistry that had sizzled between the two of them from the very first. He had meant to kiss her once. Well, maybe two or three times, and that was it. But as soon as he tasted the sweetness that was uniquely hers once again, as soon as she wrapped her arms around him and offered her mouth—her body—up to his, all his good, gentlemanly intentions went by the wayside.

Desire was flowing through him, fueling a want and need that matched her own. His hands seemed to have a life of their own. And she didn't mind one bit as he found her soft curves. First, through her clothes, and then underneath. Her nipples pearled as he unfastened her bra and shoved the fabric of her sweater aside. And when feeling her silky skin wasn't enough and he had to see her, she let him do that, too. Lifting her arms so he could tug the lightweight cardigan and matching sweater off, she let the bra fall down her arms and helped him remove his own shirt.

Then they were kissing again, right there against the wall. Her breasts nestled against the hardness of his chest. His hands moved beneath the fabric of her skirt, exploring the silky smoothness of her inner thighs, cupping her buttocks, hauling her against him as she pressed herself up, rocking against him, leaving him with absolutely no doubt about what she wanted. What they both wanted now. And then her hands were on his fly, his jeans were sliding down. Her panties were coming off. As was her skirt.

He was fumbling with the condom he'd carried in his wallet for what seemed like forever, and then they were one. Her soft groan echoed in the room, and she was climaxing, opening herself up, inviting him deeper still. That swiftly, he catapulted over the edge, shuddering. Their breath noisy and rough, they clung together. And still he wanted more. Much more.

Making love to her was just the beginning to him. But already for her, the regrets were surfacing. He felt it in the way she tensed, even before he saw it in her wary amber eyes. He could tell by the way she was looking at him that she thought this was just a casual thing for him. Something that probably happened—in her erroneous estimation—all the time. When the truth was he had never been affected like this. He could tell she was chalking this up as yet another in a long line of personal mistakes on her part. But he didn't see that giving in to the ardor between them so quickly had been a mistake. "Janey," he said, unsure where to start or what to say that wouldn't sound like some sort of line under the circumstances.

"Let's not ruin this by talking about it, Thad."

Not talking about it was what would ruin it.

She bent and swooped up her clothes, even as she pulled ever so cautiously and discreetly away. "I'm sure you think this was meant to be," she said in a voice so cool and practical it stung. "On one level, so do I." Her manner as composed as her voice, she put on her bra and panties, then her sweater and skirt. "But the mature part of me knows this isn't going to solve anything." She slipped on her sandals, too.

"Oh, I don't know about that," Thad drawled, trying to inject some lightheartedness back into a situation that was turning way too grave way too fast. "I think it helped clarify matters immensely," he said, trying hard to find the irony of the situation. Janey might fill him with the urgent need to possess her, but right now all he had managed to do was fill her with doubts.

"Right," Janey cut him off before he could continue. "When it comes to you, I seem to lack all common sense." She shook her head, her regret obvious. She went to find her shoulder bag and car keys. "I have to get back home."

Although he was loath to let her run away like this, Thad reluctantly conceded that Janey needed time to reflect, sort out her feelings and probably examine his. And on that score, as she reached the door, he caught her by the hand once again and let her know where he stood, too.

He waited until he had her full attention then looked deep into her eyes. "If you think I'm going to lose interest in you now that we've both satisfied our curiosities and made love, sweetheart, you need to think again."

"MOM, CAN WE GET season tickets to the Storm games this year?" Chris said as the two of them arrived at the bakery the following morning. Because it was just a hop, skip, and a jump to the middle school where he attended summer school, Chris would eat breakfast and do more math homework there, while Janey put the first of the three cakes she had to bake today into the oven before he headed off on his skate-board.

While Janey got out the milk and cereal for Chris from the store refrigerator, he plopped a pamphlet down in front of her, detailing the costs. It didn't take Janey long to notice that a pair of first-tier tickets for all forty-two home games would cost close to five thousand dollars. The ones in the nosebleed section weren't all that much cheaper.

"Actually, honey, since your uncle Joe is going to be playing on the Storm this year, I think we can get some free tickets to the games through him." At least Janey hoped that was the case. She would have to see.

"For every home game?"

"That, I don't know about. But for some, I'm sure."

"But I wanted to see all the home games and some of the away games, too," Chris complained.

"A lot of them will be on television," Janey soothed.

Chris scowled his disappointment. "I wanted to go in person."

"I'm sure that will be possible for some of the games. Not the ones on school nights. Your school-work comes first, remember?" Janey reminded as she got up to put some coffee on.

"What if I got a job to help pay for them?" Chris

asked, hope shining in his eyes as he eagerly worked to find a solution that would please them both.

Actually, Janey thought, you've already been offered a job. She just hadn't gotten around to telling him about it because she feared it would just make things more complicated where she and Thad Lantz were concerned. Especially now that they had both foolishly thrown caution to the wind and made love.

"You're only twelve."

"So? I could mow lawns or deliver newspapers or something. Couldn't I?"

"We'll talk about it later," Janey said.

As soon as Chris headed off to school, Janey sat back down with her coffee and her checkbook. The check she had written the night before to pay for hockey camp had seriously depleted her bank account. And though she had already paid her mortgage for the month, and could get by on what groceries she had in the pantry and refrigerator at home, she still had to pay all her utilities, and she didn't have the cash. Which left her with few options. Asking her family for money, which she frankly refused to do. Or getting a cash advance on her credit card at a hideous interest rate she would be paying off for months to come. And that, Janey thought, wouldn't help her overall situation, either.

"Don't you look like you have the weight of the world on your shoulders," Thad said.

Janey glanced up. She had been so deep in thought, she hadn't heard him come in.

She put her checkbook aside. "You wouldn't understand."

He lifted a skeptical brow as he sat down on the wooden stool Chris had occupied a few minutes before. "Putting thoughts in my head again, hmm?" he teased, looking very much like he wanted to make love to her all over again. Which in turn made her desperate to throw up some barriers between them so he couldn't get close enough to make her fall hopelessly and recklessly and impulsively in love with him.

Why not let him know where things stood? A little devil prodded her mischievously. Maybe the news of her financial troubles would send him running the way making love to her last night obviously hadn't. Wasn't that what all wildly successful men feared? A gold-digging woman who was only after the cash in their wallet? Maybe if she presented herself as a tad more mercenary and calculating.... Or just a fiscal mess. "I'm broke," she told him bluntly, and waited, with bated breath, for his reaction.

"Your shop seems to be doing great business," he observed after a minute. Looking, to her disappointment, neither put off nor surprised.

Even though she was working night and day to fill orders, she still couldn't make enough to pay herself a decent salary. Which she probably would have figured out had she not jumped into the wedding-cake-biz so recklessly. Only to, of course, regret it later.

"I had to get a small business loan to get started.

So I've got my payments on that, along with the rent for this shop, the utilities, and money it cost to put in the commercial ovens and bring this kitchen up to code.''

"And the money it's going to cost to send Chris to camp put you over the edge."

Janey made a pained face, embarrassed to always be living so close to the pecuniary edge. "Just about." How was that for unattractive?

Thad regarded her with a surprising lack of sympathy. "So let him help pay for it."

Janey blinked. She had expected Thad to remove himself from the situation as fast as possible, not offer advice. "Excuse me?"

"Obviously you haven't told your son how much you're struggling and worrying or he wouldn't be blithely asking you for things you can't afford to pay for."

"I told him we didn't have the money for camp."

"And then reversed yourself."

"Well—"

"You said nothing about how tight things really are to him. Right?"

"Right," Janey admitted reluctantly.

Thad shrugged, matter-of-fact as ever. "So my advice is to accept his offer to take responsibility for himself and pay his own way through hockey camp and ask him to take that summer job I offered him via you. I'll tear up the check you gave me last night. I haven't turned it in yet, so it hasn't been cashed.

And he can work at the practice arena two hours a day, five days a week, picking up towels in the locker room. I'll pay him minimum wage."

Janey did some quick calculations. "He still won't earn enough to pay for camp by the time school starts in the fall."

"So he'll continue to work for me weekends, and holidays during the school year until he pays off his debt. I'm sure he won't mind."

That was the problem, Janey thought. Chris wouldn't. But she would because it would mean she would be running into Thad all the time, as she ferried Chris back and forth.

"He can start today—I'll tell the assistant coaches and physical trainers to expect him. And while he's at it, he'll get a good look behind the scenes and see how much work professional hockey is, which is what you wanted in the first place, isn't it? A good dose of reality for him. Well, it doesn't get any more real than that."

THAD HAD COME into Delectable Cakes with one mission in mind—to find a way to help Janey get her life in good enough shape so she would allow herself to relax and him to romance her. "And while you're at it," he continued, cheering her on matter-of-factly, "how about a good dose of reality for yourself? You're never going to get ahead if you keep your business a small, one-person operation."

Janey sent him a predictably stormy glance before

getting up to check on the cakes baking in the oven. "I can't afford to hire help!" She began to get bowls down from the shelves.

"You can't afford not to, from the looks of it," Thad retorted frankly.

Janey brought several sticks of butter and cream cheese from the refrigerator and placed them on the counter. "Do you know how many wedding cake businesses there are in central North Carolina? Dozens! The fact I have so many orders already, after only a year here, is a real source of pride for me."

"As well it should be." Thad moved nearer. "But that doesn't mean you can't expand your business to include a wider range of product for your customers."

"You don't know what you're talking about." Looking prettier than ever in her white chef's coat and loose-fitting trousers, Janey glared at him.

He let his glance rove her upswept hair before returning to her lovely amber eyes. "I think I do," he replied, ignoring her hopelessly sexy pout. He stepped even nearer, inhaling the intoxicating fragrance of soap and confectioner's sugar clinging to her skin. "I think that's what's making you so angry. You're as afraid to take risks in business as you are in your personal life."

"I want you to get out of here right now," Janey fumed, pointing at the door.

One look at her face told Thad he was going to have to give her time to think about what he had said, and cool down before he had a chance in hell of achieving what he had initially come here to do. He needed her to muster the courage to break out of the protective cocoon she had built around herself and *live* a little.

"Have Chris at the practice arena at five o'clock," he told her gently as he prepared to take his leave.

Janey muttered something beneath her breath that sounded like an oath directed at him. A most unladylike oath, Thad noted with amusement. Damn, but he liked her spirit.

JANEY'S TEMPER WAS BURNING so hotly, it was all she could do not to kick something as Thad walked out of her bakery and climbed behind the wheel of his luxury SUV. What did he know about running a small business anyway? He was a coach with a seven-figure salary and tons of perks and no money worries at all.

And no wonder. Janey picked up the brochure Chris had left behind, and opened it up once again. Look at the price of those tickets! And the team didn't stop there. They also offered all sorts of merchandise, opportunities to pay to meet the team, and even birthday party packages for kids, complete with group ticket prices for the seats, free hot dogs and sodas for each guest, a personal visit from the mascot in the stands, and the name of the person having the birthday flashed on the Jumbotron above the ice!

Wait a minute. Janey paused, looking over the brochure once again. Nowhere did it mention anything about a cake. How could you have a birthday without a cake?

To make sure, she picked up the phone and called the Storm ticket office and smiled when her suspicions were confirmed. Thad might have helped her more than he knew.

The bell above the door rang out just as Janey was putting the phone back in the cradle. It was her brother Joe and his wife Emma. "Hey, sis, need a favor," Joe said.

Janey smiled at the two of them. They were such a handsome couple, Joe with his light brown hair and golden eyes, and Emma with her dark brown chin-length hair and wide-set dark green eyes. "The wives of Storm players are putting together a cookbook, proceeds of which will go to charity," Emma explained, looking every bit the elegant heiress, next to her star athlete husband. "Each member of the team is expected to contribute his or her favorite recipe."

"And mine is your chicken gumbo," Joe said, flashing a warm familial smile her way. "So would you mind coughing up the recipe for me and showing Emma how to make it?"

"So I can honestly say it's something I've made for Joe?" Emma continued hopefully.

"No problem," Janey promised, knowing Emma was an ace wedding planner but as much a novice in the kitchen as her youngest brother was.

"Would tonight be too soon?" Joe asked hopefully.

"Tonight would be fine," Janey promised, knowing the busier she kept herself the better. She didn't want to be thinking about Thad Lantz any more than she already was.

"THIS IS SO AWESOME," Chris said when Janey drove him over to the Storm practice arena later that afternoon. "You're so great for arranging a job for me."

Janey only wished she could take the credit. She hadn't seen her son looking so happy since she didn't remember when. And it was all due to Thad and his influence on Chris. "It was Coach Lantz's idea," Janey revealed casually.

"Really?" Excitement shone in Chris's eyes.

Janey nodded. There went her son, reading too much into a simple act of kindness again. Just the way she had wanted to read too much into Thad's making love to her. Just because she and Thad were compatible physically didn't mean they were suited to each other in every other way. What had happened had been reckless and passionate, and done without much thought to anything but that very moment in time. Which was just the way Thad had wanted it. And her, too, of course. She didn't have time to even consider getting involved in a romantic liaison. She had her hands full just being a mother and a businesswoman.

Thad was waiting for Chris when Janey walked Chris into the arena. "If you want, I can see he gets a ride home," Thad said politely, as Janey handed off her son.

Chris's eyes lit up with the possibilities, as several Storm players walked out from the locker room, gym bags in hand.

Janey shook her head no, avoiding looking directly into Thad's eyes. "Thanks, but I can get him on my way home from the shop," she said in the officiously pleasant tone she used with customers. "Seven o'clock?"

"Right." Looking as if he either didn't notice or didn't care about the polite wall she was erecting between them, Thad turned his attention to her son. He clapped his hand on Chris's shoulder and led him on inside the practice arena. "Come on, sport. Let me introduce you to the rest of the coaching staff...."

Telling herself Thad's equally neutral attitude toward her was for the best, Janey went back to her store, and continued working on her proposal to expand her business. If she could get this, she would be in the black in no time, and she would be able to hire more help, as well. And the ironic thing of course, was that she had Thad Lantz to thank for her idea. Had he not pushed her so hard that morning, had her temper not skyrocketed, she knew she wouldn't have picked up the brochure or been thinking that way.

All too soon, it was time to go back to the arena to get Chris. There were only four cars left in the lot. One of them was Thad's SUV.

With Chris nowhere in sight, Janey figured she had

no choice but to go on inside. To her surprise, Chris was out on the ice with Thad, working on his shooting. Both were wearing skates and looked like the natural athletes they were. "You want to keep both hands high on the stick when you're getting ready to shoot off a pass," Thad was explaining, his back to Janey.

"How come?" Chris asked earnestly, while Janey tried hard not to notice what broad, muscular shoulders and a nice backside the jeans-clad Thad possessed.

"Because it's easier to move your lower hand down on the center of the stick, where it needs to be situated when the pass comes, than to move it back up..." Thad said, gently coaching her son. "See, the whole thing is quickness and control...."

While Janey watched from the short row of bleachers that surrounded the practice ice, Thad continued explaining then had Chris fire off a practice shot. It was the best shot Janey had ever seen her son make.

"That's so much easier that way!" Chris shouted enthusiastically as he looked up at Thad in adulation. "You're a really good teacher, you know that? Not just at hockey, but math, too."

Thad clamped a paternal hand on Chris's shoulders, looking at that moment more like a devoted father to her son than instructor slash employer. The mutual respect and admiration between them made Janey's heart ache. "That's what coaching is—teaching," Thad told her son humbly.

It was more than that, Janey thought, gratitude flowing through her.

Chris'd had a lot of people coaching him over the years, in both his schoolwork and sports. None had made such a quick impact on him as Thad. Whether she wanted to admit it or not, there was something special going on there. Something Chris hadn't even had with his dad...who, as much as he had loved Chris, hadn't possessed a lot of patience when it came to teaching Chris anything, athletic or otherwise.

Catching sight of Janey, Thad waved and guided Chris in that direction, too. "Chris finished his work early, so I put him through a few drills on the ice." He looked at her questioningly. "I hope you don't mind."

"It's fine." Janey smiled at him awkwardly. "Thank you."

Thad looked over at Chris. "You know where to put your pads in the locker room?"

Chris nodded and went off to get his shoes.

"You're looking...cheerful," Thad noted as he skated over to the wall that edged the practice ice.

That's because she now had hope of expanding her business as quickly as she needed.

He regarded her with narrowed eyes. "I thought you might still be ticked off at me—for this morning."

Janey shrugged, not too proud to admit, "From a business perspective, you were dead-on."

''And from a personal perspective?'' Thad prodded. Janey hesitated, not sure what to say.

''Best we not go there again?'' he guessed.

She nodded, her pulse kicking up another notch. She couldn't say why exactly, but she only wanted him to admire her. Thus far, a lot of what he had seen of her was not exactly her best side. Which made it all the more wondrous that he was still so attracted to her.

''If there's anything I can do,'' Thad offered warmly, as he came around the wall and closed the distance between them.

Here it was. Her golden opportunity to use her in with him to help her get what she wanted. But if she did that, would it be much different from going to her family for help? Somehow, Janey didn't think so. ''Thanks, but I can manage on my own,'' she said, her body registering the heat as he took a seat beside her. She slanted him a sidelong glance. ''I am curious about one thing, though. This is your off-season. I'd think you would want to get away from coaching. As much as possible anyway. And yet here you are, giving tips to Chris.''

Thad shrugged his broad shoulders. They were sitting so close his arm nudged hers. ''We had time to kill. And I enjoy working with him. All kids for that matter.'' He turned to her and looked deep into her eyes.

She had the feeling he was thinking about kissing

her—and making love with her—again. Her throat tightened. "How come?"

Thad hesitated. "Maybe because it reminds me of my youth. Playing sports was the best part of growing up for me. And if I can take that experience and give it back to the next generation…"

Janey understood. She was a baker for the same reason, because she had loved doing it when she was growing up. And still did. "Well, it's got to give you good karma, that's for sure."

Thad smiled over at her. And then Chris came bursting out of the locker room, ready to take on what was left of his day.

"THAT WASN'T HARD at all," Emma murmured, as the four of them finished off the chicken gumbo Janey had helped them make for the team cookbook.

Joe grinned. "You're right. 'Cause if it's easy enough for me to put together, anyone can do it.' Taking his new wife by the hand, he pushed his chair back from the table and tugged her over onto his lap.

Chris made a face, and excused himself, muttering something about "crazy newlyweds," before heading up to his room to work on his math homework.

"Hey—if you need some more help with that—" Joe called after his nephew helpfully.

"I'll call Coach Lantz," Chris yelled back. "'Cause he's the one with all the right answers!"

"No kidding." Joe settled back in his chair.

"So how is it going with the new team?" Janey

asked her brother curiously. She knew Joe had wanted to play on his hometown hockey team forever, and now he finally had the chance. If she didn't somehow muck things up for him.

Joe beamed the way he always did when talking about hockey. "The team hasn't practiced together as a group yet 'cause it's still the off-season, but everyone I've met, and the training staff, have been fantastic."

Janey was relieved to hear that.

Joe gave her a curious glance. "You seem to be getting along with Thad Lantz, too."

The way he said that triggered a silent alarm in Janey's head. Suddenly, she knew it wasn't just the need for cooking expertise that had her brother at her home that evening. "You heard from Mac, didn't you?" Janey guessed soberly.

"That you were seen kissing him? Yes," Joe revealed grimly, "I did."

"Joe—" Emma gave her husband a light warning punch in the shoulder. "You promised you were not going to bring this up!"

"I'm not giving Janey a hard time." Joe held up both hands in surrender as he ignored his wife's chastisement. He assessed Janey pointedly. "I'm just asking where she stands with all this."

That was just it. Janey didn't know. "We're getting to know each other," she said finally, telling as much of the truth as she could, without inviting even more meddling in her private life.

"As friends or something more?" Joe demanded bluntly, earning himself another censuring frown from his wife.

Janey looked her brother straight in the eye, figuring she owed Joe this much, since he was now going to be working under Thad's direction. "I don't know yet," she stated as evenly as she could.

"Okay," Emma interceded briskly, with a savvy wedding planner's tact. "Enough questions. We've got to get home." Emma leaped off Joe's lap. "As soon as we help with the dishes anyway."

Janey waved off their offer of help. "I can get 'em. You two lovebirds go enjoy yourself." Heaven knew someone in the family should, and right now Joe was the only one of her siblings who was attached.

"Just be careful," Joe warned Janey at the door. "He's a good guy."

"But?" Janey prodded, sensing there was more.

Worry flickered in Joe's eyes. "Since his divorce five years ago, Thad Lantz has a reputation for never getting involved with anyone for very long."

Well, that was encouraging, Janey scowled unhappily, as she finished saying goodbye, and went to do the dishes. She had just started loading the dishwasher when the doorbell rang.

Chapter Six

Thad Lantz was standing on the other side of the doorway. He looked relaxed and sexy, the hint of an evening beard lining his face. "Sorry to come by so late, but I was just making a final pass through the locker room at the practice arena, and I caught sight of this." He held up a sixth-grade math book. "I thought Chris might need it."

"Thanks." Their hands brushed as she accepted it from him.

His blue eyes glimmered with a mixture of amusement and desire. "It must have dropped out of his backpack."

Or been left deliberately, Janey thought wryly. In order to give Thad Lantz a chance to drop by? She flashed back to all the times during the dinner with his beloved uncle Joe and aunt Emma that Chris had leapt up to get the phone, or kept an eye on the door. Even hockey talk hadn't totally held her son's attention. Now, at last, she knew why. He had been expecting someone!

"Well, I've got to go grab something to eat before I head home," Thad said casually.

Janey felt herself flush with an inner warmth she could not contain. Her brows knit together. "You haven't had dinner?"

Thad shook his head. "Too busy, working on plans for the preseason."

She and Chris should not be imposing on Thad so much without giving back something in return, Janey thought, guilt flowing through her. Before she could stop herself, she found herself offering with the southern hospitality with which she had been reared, "I've got some chicken gumbo, salad, and whole wheat rolls left over from our dinner, if you'd like to stay."

"Sounds delicious." Thad flashed her a winning smile, looking as though he had expected to be invited in for dinner the whole time. He walked in, his big body filling the space. "Chicken gumbo, hmm?"

Janey nodded, unable to help but notice the sizzle between them that seemed to increase by leaps and bounds with every interaction. "It's an old family recipe with a few new twists."

His gaze roamed the length of her, taking in her bare feet, V-necked T-shirt and form-fitting shorts. "Sounds...enticing..."

Trying hard not to be affected by the intimacy of the situation, or the sensual pine fragrance of his cologne, Janey turned toward the staircase. "Just let me take this book up to Chris and let him know you're here."

Rather than look irritated at the fact they would

soon have a twelve-year-old chaperone, Thad seemed pleased.

Another point in his favor, Janey thought with a rueful sigh. How was she ever going to get this man out of her heart and her mind if he kept being so darn admirable? Usually, the fact she had a son put men off. Not that she was interested in men in any case. Her life was fine as it was. Or it would be, as soon as she got her financial house in order. Thanks to the much-needed push Thad had given her that morning, she now was working on a brilliant plan to do just that.

Chris's door was ajar. He was lying facedown on the bed, fast asleep, a book about hockey greats clutched to his chest. So much for working on the math that was due by Friday, Janey thought, disappointed but not surprised.

"Everything okay?" Thad asked as Janey came back downstairs. As always he saw too much of what she was thinking and feeling.

She led the way into her homey country kitchen and dished up some salad for Thad. "You may as well know, I think he left that book at the practice arena on purpose."

Thad leaned against the counter, arms folded in front of him, and continued to survey her thoughtfully. "I figured as much. It's one of the reasons I waited so late to come by. I didn't want to intrude on whatever you had planned for this evening."

"Thank you." Unable to look into his eyes any longer, without thinking about kissing him again, she dropped her glance to the strong column of his throat and the crisp curling hair visible in the open V of his knit shirt. "Both for being so understanding and biding your time."

Even if my entire family has put you in one heck of an awkward situation. Not just once. But over and over again.

He quirked a brow at the increasingly pink contours of her face, seeming to know intuitively there was something else she wasn't telling. "Anything else happen here tonight I should know about?" he asked curiously.

Janey handed him the bottle of ranch salad dressing. "It's my brothers again."

Thad sat down at the kitchen table. "Which one?" he asked.

"It doesn't matter." Janey put the gumbo and bread in front of him, too. "They're all insanely protective of me. And just so you know, their continuing 'concern' has nothing to do with you and everything to do with me."

"Because you eloped when you were just nineteen after knowing Ty for all of five days," Thad guessed.

Boy, he had a good memory, Janey thought as she sat down opposite him at the small round kitchen table. She traced the pattern on the glossy white-and-green ceramic-tiled top. "The frustrating thing for me is that they don't have any reason to worry these days, because that's never going to happen again." She looked up and gazed into his eyes, not sure why she wanted Thad to know this, just realizing that she did.

"I have no intention of marrying anyone." She had been too miserable the first time, had been forced to work too hard not to show it.

He gave her the once-over. "Never?"

Janey shook her head, hanging on to her independence with everything she had. "I'm not going to put myself or my son in a position where we are hurt again," she stated clearly.

"Ty hurt his son?"

Once again, she had said too much. But having blurted out what she had, she had no choice but to go on, lest Thad get the wrong idea about what she meant. "He would have," she said quietly, "had I not covered for him so much."

"I don't get it."

But he wanted to, Janey thought, relieved finally to have someone she could confide in who wouldn't judge her or tell her what a reckless fool she had been for ever having hitched her wagon to Ty's in the first place. "Ty loved Chris as much as he was capable of loving anyone or anything, but Ty's number one priority was still Ty. If something better came along— and it usually did—Ty wouldn't hesitate to cancel plans with Chris. It didn't seem to matter if it was Chris's birthday or any other holiday," she related miserably. "If Ty got a call to go avalanche-skiing— he was out of there. Whether he got paid as a guide or not. And that's why we had so much trouble paying our bills, because Ty was cavalier about money."

"And Chris never guessed what was going on."

Thad looked as angry and disapproving as Janey had felt.

Janey flushed. "I couldn't tell him that the birthday gift he thought came from his dad, came from me. Or that Ty had taken off on what turned out to be a social ski trip rather than spend Christmas with him. It would have devastated him." Just as it had devastated her.

"So you covered." Thad reached over and took her hand protectively in his.

"And covered and covered until Ty was killed in that avalanche, skiing where he had no business being," Janey murmured softly, relaxing in Thad's strong, warm grip before looking deep into his eyes. "So now you know," she finished with no small trace of disparagement. "I'm not so admirable after all."

Because an admirable person would have found a way not to have to lie to her son and everyone else she knew. An admirable person would have found a way to fix her marriage before it ever landed in such a sorry state, she thought derisively. But Thad apparently did not agree with her punishing self-assessment.

"You have nothing to be ashamed about," he told her sternly, holding her gaze. "You held your family together, at great personal sacrifice. That's more than most would do."

What was it Joe had just told her about Thad? *Since his divorce five years ago, he has a reputation for never getting involved with any woman for long…* Maybe it was time Thad shared some of what was in his heart and on his mind with her, too. "Is that what happened in your marriage?" she asked quietly. "Your wife left when you would have held things together."

For a moment, Janey thought Thad wasn't going to answer. Finally, he said, "I met Renee when I was twenty-nine. She had just had a baby and the guy had left her for someone else—he had no interest whatsoever in his son, Bobby. The jerk wouldn't let anyone else adopt Bobby, either. But I stepped in anyway, and became a father to Bobby, and a husband to Renee. I had this fantasy I could solve all her problems and make her happy, keep the two of them safe."

So he had been a white knight, riding gallantly to the rescue, even then. "Did you love her?" Did he still?

Thad shrugged his broad shoulders carelessly. "At the time I thought I did. Now, I'm not so sure it wasn't just the situation that drew me."

Janey bit her lip uncertainly. "I don't understand."

He leaned toward her matter-of-factly. "I like being needed, being there for someone in an essential way. I find that very personally satisfying."

"Which is why you like coaching both kids and adults," Janey guessed, thinking he certainly had found the right profession.

"Right. Anyway, we were together for four years, and during that time Renee became increasingly dissatisfied with our financial situation," he recalled, his eyes darkening. "I was sure I was going to make it to the major league coaching circles—all the signs were there—but Renee had no such assurance. Bottom line, she was not happy being 'the wife of a minor leaguer' I think is how she put it. So she left me and moved to Portland, forcing me to cut off all contact with Bobby, who was five by that time. I could have sued her for visitation rights, but I knew it would be difficult at best for me to see Bobby. And by then Renee had made her dreams come true by marrying someone wealthy that even I could see loved her and Bobby. So I did what was best in the long run and agreed to cut all ties with Bobby.''

Janey's heart went out to him for having been put in such a no-win situation. ''And you regret it.''

Thad shrugged, suddenly appearing weary to his very soul. ''I know I hurt Bobby,'' he said in a low, remorse-filled voice. ''And I can't forgive myself for that.''

Janey understood. To see a child you loved in pain was absolutely unbearable. To see it and know you were at least partially responsible was even worse. She sensed that Thad—like herself—would do whatever he had to do to prevent any more distress. ''Is he happy now?''

Thad nodded, the tension in his broad shoulders easing slightly. ''Renee and I still have some mutual friends—and they've assured me he really is.'' As their gazes locked, his lips tightened with determination. ''Nevertheless, I've promised myself I will never take a kid into my heart again while dating the mom, or become a surrogate father to him or her and then abandon him if and when things don't work out." He shook his head regretfully. "I've walked that road before and it's just too damn painful."

"WAS COACH LANTZ HERE last night?" Chris asked Thursday morning over breakfast.

"He brought your math book to you around ten. Funny thing," Janey drawled, "you leaving it at the arena."

Chris blushed and ducked his head.

Guilty as charged, Janey thought. Her son had done it on purpose. Was he that desperate for a male influence in his life? And why weren't his five uncles— who all cared about him deeply—sufficient? Why was Chris so drawn to Thad, unless it was for the same complicated, inexplicable reasons she was? Because somehow, just being with him felt so right. Predestined, somehow.

"I'll have to thank him," Chris murmured into his glass of orange juice.

"Yes, I think you should," Janey said with a pointed look as she ladled scrambled eggs onto Chris's plate. Regardless of the sticky emotional circumstances, good manners needed to be used. "So how is your math homework coming? Are you going to be able to finish all of next week's assignments before tomorrow?"

His sheepishness fading, Chris nodded. "There's just one section I don't understand."

"Maybe you could ask your teacher to help you

with it before you leave summer school today,'' Janey suggested.

Chris nodded noncommittally.

Janey dropped Chris off at school, then went to the shop and immediately telephoned the Carolina Storm's business office for an appointment the following week. She was told the person who made such appointments wasn't in, but they would get back to her. So Janey left her name and number, put the batter for two cakes in the oven that needed to be completed that day—and started plotting out the decorations of the line of birthday cakes she planned to offer the following week.

The afternoon was filled with half a dozen wedding cake appointments to select, plus the completion of the cakes she was working on. She dropped Chris at the arena for work at five, delivered one cake to her mother at The Wedding Inn, then took another to a four-star hotel in Raleigh. En route back to Holly Springs, she got caught in rush-hour traffic and knew she wasn't going to make it to the practice arena by seven to pick up Chris. She tried calling her siblings and her mother on her cell—none of them were answering. Finally, in desperation she called the arena office. Thad answered the phone. Hearing her problem, he quickly offered to take Chris home.

''Really, he could take a cab,'' Janey said, hating to impose. If it weren't for the fact Chris would have to cross a major highway on foot and journey a good four miles, she would have had him ride his skateboard home.

"Don't be ridiculous," he scoffed, his warm familiar voice sending tingles down her spine. "I'll see you later." He hung up before she had a chance to reply.

CHRIS AND THAD WERE sitting at the kitchen table, their heads bowed together over a textbook when Janey walked in, looking hot and tired and utterly frazzled from the events of her day. If she was surprised to see the two of them sitting there, working on Chris's math homework, she didn't show it. "How's it going?"

"Good. I'm starting to get it now," Chris said. He looked at Janey earnestly. "When's dinner, Mom? I'm starved." Chris turned to Thad expectantly. "Want to stay?"

"Chris!" Janey exclaimed, horrified by the pressure her son was exerting.

"Really, you do not have to issue an invitation," Thad said, already rising politely, even though he wanted nothing more than to stay and spend another evening with her.

"But we got plenty!" Chris interrupted eagerly. "Mom, he's hungry, too. You should have heard his stomach growling before you came in, and he *looked* hungry, too. You like spaghetti, don't you, Coach?"

Thad nodded slowly, looked into Janey's eyes. She looked torn between amusement and acquiescence to what increasingly seemed like a losing battle—at least where her son was concerned. And there was something else there, too. Whatever she was afraid of—

when it came to the attraction building between them—she was obviously as enthralled by it as he was.

"YOU REALLY DON'T have to help me with the dishes," Janey said two hours later, after Chris had gone upstairs to shower and get ready for bed. Thad had been a good sport, but they had imposed on him quite enough for one night.

"Then how about walking me out?" Thad asked.

She could tell by the way he was looking at her that he wanted to talk to her privately. Truth was, she wanted to talk to him, too. "Can't find your SUV, hmm?" she teased, not sure why this should suddenly feel so much like a date when it clearly wasn't.

Thad shrugged his broad shoulders lazily. "Always good to have backup." He gave her an ardent glance that upped her pulse another notch. "You know what I mean?"

They shut the door behind them and strolled down the walk, away from the yellow glow of the porch light to the curb. Instead of circling around to the driver side, Thad leaned against the front passenger side of his SUV.

She looked away, realizing she was on the verge of falling in love with him. The prospect of depending on him and his solid, reassuring presence in her life absolutely terrified her. "I'm sorry about the way Chris put you on the spot tonight," Janey said softly, determined to keep things on an even keel. "He's not usually so pushy, but as we both know, when it comes to you he's got this hero-worship thing going.''

"The admiration is mutual, believe me," Thad replied huskily.

Janey looked into his face, saw the sincerity reflected there.

His profile was bathed in silvery moonlight and the glow of the streetlamps overhead, making him look all the more handsome. Janey splayed her hands across the hardness of his chest. She loved the strength and warmth of him, the gentleness in his touch, the sexiness of his kisses, the reckless way he had made love with her, and the way he still refused—ever so subtly—to let her back away.

Thad hooked an arm about her waist and drew her near. "Thank you for dinner," he whispered, holding her close and studying her upturned face.

"My pleasure," Janey murmured back, wanting to go to bed with him again so much. Not that they'd ever made it to the bed that first time....

Thad stroked his hands through her hair. "I think Chris felt sorry for me," he confessed in a low, teasing tone. "Being a single guy and all. At least, he kept telling me how great a cook you were."

Janey blushed, knowing—as did Thad—that Chris had a little matchmaking in his blood. "He mistakenly thinks the way to a man's heart is through his stomach," Janey said wryly.

Thad guided her around, so her back was to the SUV door. He moved forward, until their bodies fit as snugly as a lock and key. She could feel his arousal and recalled with stunning clarity what a demanding and yet ultimately giving lover he had been. "Where would he get that idea?"

"His uncles, probably," Janey murmured, aware her body was burning everywhere they touched. Her nipples were aching. Her thighs were liquid, weak. Hanging on to her self-control by a thread, she finished playfully, "None of them can cook one bit."

"Hmm." He scored his thumb across her bottom lip. "So, in other words, being helpless works in attracting females?"

Heat started low in her body and welled up through her chest. "Depends on which female you want to attract."

"Only one." He leaned closer and pressed a kiss to her flushed cheek, a gentlemen to the end. "You."

"Thad—"

He tightened his arms on her possessively and looked down at her with all the love she had ever dreamed of. "I know you probably think I'm hanging around too much—"

He fastened his lips on hers. And once he demanded her surrender, once she felt the hardness of his body pressing resolutely against hers, there was no stopping with just one kiss. He stroked, he teased, he caressed, until she surged against him, threading her hands through his hair. Until she was kissing him back more recklessly and wantonly and completely than ever before.

Janey tilted her head back, stroking his tongue with hers, relishing his warmth and his strength and the myriad sensations coursing through her body. She wanted him...so much. And they were out on the street, standing in front of her house, in plain view of any of her neighbors who might look out their windows, or just happen to walk or drive along.

Moaning her frustration that Thad had come into her life at the wrong time, Janey broke off the heady kiss. She rested her brow against his chin, eyes closed, a complex tangle of feelings fighting for control inside her. Thad drew back slightly, kissing her forehead, her cheek, the tip of her nose, the delicate shell of her ear.

She caught her breath as his tongue traced the nape of her neck. It was all she could do not to melt right there on the sidewalk. She groaned again, this time in frustration. "If you keep this up, people will start to talk."

"Can I help it if I spend all my time daydreaming up excuses to be close to you?" he challenged with a gallantry that kindled her senses.

"We have to think of the example we're setting for Chris," she protested unevenly.

He tunneled his hands through her hair and looked down at her, affection in his eyes, his face still tantalizingly close to hers. "The best example there is would be to show your son how a man acts when he is in serious courting mode."

Janey's heart took a little leap as she thought about the implications of that. Awareness shimmered between them, more potent with every second that passed. "*Are* you courting me—seriously?" Janey demanded breathlessly.

Did she want him to? She had said she didn't ever want to get married again. Until tonight, until now, that had certainly been true.... But it wasn't. Not anymore.

His eyes held a quiet steadiness that made her tremble. "Kiss me again and tell me what you think."

She rose up on tiptoe and met him halfway. His kiss was brimming with feeling—and a hunger she hadn't known she could possess surged through her veins. Her lips softened beneath his as he kissed her long and hard and deep. She opened her mouth, wanting, needing more from this yearning that called to the deepest reaches of her being. The sure pressure of his lips felt so warm, so right as she met that melding of hearts and souls with the pent-up passion of a lifetime, and the fear of the recklessness and regrets still to come. She clung to him, her fingers digging into his shoulders, her breasts pillowed against his chest as she passionately returned kiss for kiss. Their hearts were pounding, pulses racing. She was trembling with the effort at restraint. And so was he, she noted dizzily, as—mindful of where they were—they slowly, reluctantly let the kiss end again.

For a moment, they simply stood there, breathing hard, gazing at each other.

"That felt pretty serious," Janey whispered finally, luxuriating in the feel of the arms still wrapped securely around her.

"Good." Thad looked down into her face, his blue eyes brimming with an emotion he made no effort to hide. "Because it is."

JANEY WALKED BACK into the house, still feeling dazed from Thad's kisses. She went straight to the kitchen, and the dishes she had left soaking in the sink. Chris came down the stairs. He was wearing a Carolina Storm T-shirt and pajama pants. His hair was slicked wetly back from his face. And in the light of the kitchen, Janey could see a few long blond whiskers on his chin. Soon he too would be needing to shave. He really was growing up so fast....

"Coach leave?" Chris asked, plucking an apple from the fruit bowl on the counter.

Janey nodded, aware her knees were still a little wobbly.

"You sure were outside a long time talking to him," Chris observed.

How had he known that? "I thought you were in the shower!"

"For ten minutes," Chris responded with the authority of one who knew the facts. "You were outside for thirty!"

Janey blushed self-consciously. Had it been that long? She had known the man could kiss and that he had a way of making time stand still when they were together, but she had no idea they'd been outside kissing for that long.

"Were you kissing him, Mom?" Chris asked her sincerely. "I just ask because it looked like you were and I want you to know if that's what was happening out there it's okay with me.''

"It is?'' Janey ascertained slowly, blushing all the more. She had always figured he would protest her involvement with anyone other than his late father, when it came right down to it.

"Yeah.'' Chris polished the apple on the front of his T-shirt. "He's an awesome dude. You should be with somebody like that. Especially after—''

"After what?'' Janey asked, as Chris ducked his head shyly and didn't go on.

"Well, I was just wondering.'' Chris paused, at the moment looking so very much like Ty as he looked Janey straight in the eye. "Dad never really made you happy, did he?''

It was Janey's turn to duck her head and flush. "What makes you think that?'' she asked uncomfortably, not sure whether she should continue painting a rosy picture that hadn't really existed or treat her son like the grown-up he was becoming and simply tell the truth.

Chris's matter-of-fact attitude and straight talk helped her decide.

"Because you were always so tense and kind of fake-happy when Dad was around. When you're with Coach Lantz, like tonight, you're always smiling or laughing and so is he, and your face kind of lights up or something when he comes in the room. I always thought that kind of stuff was just in the movies, but…''

"I wasn't aware I was so transparent," she said, embarrassed.

"Hey. You feel what you feel. If you like someone you just gotta go with it. You know?"

Janey made a show of clearing her throat. "What are you trying to say here, Chris?" As if it weren't already perfectly obvious.

Chris gave her a reassuring pat on the shoulder. "I want you to know it's okay with me if you start dating again or even want to get married or something."

He really was so smitten with the idea of the three of them becoming a family. Janey only wished she didn't have the same secret wedding wish, because there was no telling how Thad felt about her. Yes, Thad desired her. He liked spending time with her and Chris. He had even liked making love with her, on the one occasion they had risked it. But beyond that? When Thad said he was courting her seriously, how did he expect that courtship to end? In something as enduring as marriage or just in a prolonged love affair? It was impossible for her to tell. All Janey knew for certain was that she couldn't begin to predict the future now, any more than she ever had.

"Well, I'm glad you think that," Janey said slowly, aware one of her problems had just been solved, because now she knew exactly how to broach what she needed to tell Chris. She smiled at her son, hoping he would be as happy about this as she was. "Because tomorrow evening Thad and I are going on our first official date."

Chapter Seven

Thad had always known Janey was one hell of a sexy woman, and when he arrived to pick her up for their date the next evening, she looked it in a spaghetti-strap chantilly lace dress several shades darker than her hair. It fell to just below her knees, and was cinched in at the waist with a ribbon belt he immediately yearned to undo. Her long sexy legs were encased in sheer dark stockings, and high-heeled sandals added three inches to her height. Making her, he thought, just that much easier to kiss...

"You look...amazing," Thad murmured as she ushered him inside her home. Everything about her was perfection, from the soft chestnut waves tumbling down around her shoulders, to the subdued rose lipstick on her lips and the smoky taupe shadow on her lids. And she smelled fantastic, too. Like expensive perfume that filled his senses and beckoned a man to a woman's bed. The only problem being, they weren't going home to his bed but to a party for his sister and her bridegroom. So, unfortunately the ravishing was going to have to wait.

"I think she looks pretty good, too," Chris said proudly as he popped up behind Janey, eager as always to talk to Thad. "For a mom, I mean," Chris finished hastily.

Thad smiled at Chris, then turned back to Janey. He couldn't stop looking at her, and she seemed to feel the same way about him. "She looks amazing, period," Thad murmured as Janey flashed a shyly appreciative gaze his way, then gathered her evening purse and keys. Unable to help but put her mom hat on once more before they headed out the door, she said in an *I don't want any trouble while I'm gone* voice, "Now, about your evening…"

Chris held up a silencing palm, adroitly cutting off whatever speech she had been about to make. "Not to worry, Mom," Chris said with a look that promised he would be on his best behavior in the absence of parental supervision. "I've got my evening all planned out, too. I'm going to start getting my stuff ready for camp on Sunday, and watch the hockey video Uncle Joe gave me, take a shower, get something to eat and head to bed. So you can come in whenever you want because I won't be waiting up."

Flushing, Janey avoided Thad's gaze. "That's very considerate of you, honey. But I'll be home by midnight, I promise."

Chris shrugged, looking as unwilling for his mother to have to cut short her fun on some arbitrary time clock as Thad was. "Don't rush on my account," Chris repeated.

Janey rolled her eyes, then leaned forward to kiss the top of his head. "See ya."

"See ya!" Chris hugged her then darted off, turning when he was nearly to the kitchen. "'Bye, Coach!"

"'Bye, Chris." Thad smiled at Chris, thinking what a great kid he was, then held the door for Janey and escorted her down the sidewalk to his waiting SUV.

As expected, Janey's embarrassed apology wasn't long in coming. "My brothers aren't that bad when it comes to interfering in my love life," Janey complained.

Thad leaned closer, pressed a light kiss to her cheek and whispered in her ear, "I think it's kind of cute. The way he sort of keeps pushing us together."

Janey paused next to the passenger door and waited for him to open it for her. A becoming pink flush staining her cheeks, she chided ruefully, "You say that now."

And although Thad would like nothing better, the thinking side of him knew it wasn't the wisest course to take. Janey needed to know he wasn't just interested in her for the sex—which was, admittedly, by far the most incredible, physically invigorating and emotionally satisfying he'd ever had.

Rather, he wanted to spend time with her, discover everything about her there was to know—and tell her everything in return—until they were as close as it was possible for a man and woman to be.

Not that it was going to be easy, of course. Thad was only beginning to get past his own reservations about getting involved with a woman with a child. And Thad knew Janey still had her defenses up. He could tell by the way she looked at him sometimes that she feared the sizzle between them was going to fade, as soon as the novelty passed. But Thad knew that aspect was likely to only get stronger and stronger with time. As were their feelings for each other. Because the more he knew about Janey Hart Campbell, the more he liked—to the point he was beginning not to be able to imagine the rest of his life without her. Or her son.

The trick, of course, would be to get Janey to feel the very same way about him. But Thad had managed much more difficult tasks in his life. All he had to do to accomplish what he wanted was to keep them both in the game until the victorious finish.

"YOU'VE GOT TO SAVE ME," Molly told Thad soon after he and Janey walked into the crowd of guests congregated at The Wedding Inn to celebrate Molly and Johnny's wedding.

"And why would I need to do that?" Thad asked, as Janey looked across the room at his sister's new husband. Johnny was clad in a handsome summer suit and speaking to a group of guys his own age.

"Because," Molly retorted, looking pretty but petulant in a pastel pink dress with a fitted bodice and full calf-length skirt, "Mom has the bright idea we're going to say our vows in front of everyone." Her lower lip slid out another half inch. "I wouldn't be surprised if she had a wedding gown waiting in the wings somewhere."

Thad laced a comforting arm around his younger sister's shoulders. "You are her only daughter. Would it really hurt to humor her about this?"

"Yes." Molly folded her arms in front of her. "Having to endure this reception is bad enough, without going through some cornball reenactment of our vows."

An odd thing to say about your wedding, Janey thought, even if you weren't much for sentiment. And she didn't necessarily believe Molly was that pragmatic, even if she were acting so at the moment. "Does Johnny feel this way, too?" Janey asked Molly.

Molly shrugged. "Probably, but he's too polite to say so."

"You know..." Thad drawled, trying—like Janey—to tease the bride into a better mood. "In some circles civil behavior is actually considered a virtue."

Molly made a resentful face. "Thank you, Mr. Manners." She slipped beneath an air-conditioning vent and fanned herself. "Do you mind?" she said when Thad followed. "You're blocking my air."

Thad frowned, looking more worried now than perplexed. "You have got to calm down," he told his little sister sternly.

Her cheeks pinkening all the more, Molly looked at Janey for her reaction.

"Your brother's right," Janey said gently. "You look all flushed."

Worse, Molly was wearing her heart—or perhaps what was lacking in it—out for everyone to see. It had only taken Janey a few minutes to see that even when Molly and Johnny were walking around to greet the guests together, they seemed to be avoiding eye contact with each other. And there was always a discreet space between them of a foot or more. They weren't holding hands or brushing up against each other or smiling adoringly at each other from time to time. They were simply working the room, politely, efficiently. Whether because they were nervous or there was something really wrong with this picture, Janey didn't know. And neither did Thad.

Lionel came up to Thad. "Steal you for a moment, son? We need to talk about the champagne toast with Johnny's folks and figure out how it's going to go."

"Go, go!" Looking pained but relieved, Molly shooed them away.

Thad and his stepfather moved off.

"Honestly, I can barely breathe because the bodice of this dress is so tight," Molly complained, the moment they were alone. She looked at Janey. "Will you help me loosen it for just a minute?"

Janey knew a ploy to escape the party when she saw one. "Sure," Janey said easily, aware the bodice did look a little snug over Molly's breasts. But not so much it would be causing aggravating discomfort.

"Let's go upstairs to the bridal dressing room." They would have privacy there.

To avoid having to stop and speak to arriving guests every other step, they slipped through the back hall, past the kitchen and to the service stairs. Once inside the luxurious suite, Janey obliged Molly by unfastening the hook and eye and lowering the zipper on the back of her strapless silk-chiffon dress. Aware Molly still looked flushed and unhappy, she went into the adjacent bathroom, dampened a washcloth with cool water, and came back and laid it across the back of Molly's neck. "Maybe this will help cool you off."

"Thanks." Molly dropped onto the middle of the chaise lounge next to the window. She shook her head miserably. "This kind of attention is the last thing I—we—wanted. It's why we eloped in the first place."

Janey sat down next to her and took her hand. "I never realized that you were that shy," Janey said.

"I'm not." Molly studied the plain gold band on her left hand, as if wondering how it had gotten there. "I just hate the speculation. Everyone staring at me. Trying to figure out why we eloped."

Janey smiled at her gently. "I would think that at least would be obvious." Her words were meant to comfort. Instead, Molly looked stricken.

"Wh-what do you mean?" Molly demanded as she vaulted from her perch. Her dress started to slip. Frowning, Molly reached around behind her, to zip up her dress.

Janey shrugged as she stood up to lend a hand. "You're in love. You're young. Obviously a little impetuous. What else do people need to know about the situation?"

Abruptly, Molly began to relax. She looked at Janey. "That's right," she said thoughtfully. "You eloped, too."

"I'm surprised you remember that, since you were only—what—eight at the time?"

Molly removed the cool cloth from the back of her neck and gave it back to Janey. "Actually, my mom mentioned it to me when we got back from Gatlinburg. She was telling me about all the famous Holly Springs elopements. Yours created quite a stir."

Yes, it had, Janey thought as she put the cloth in the bathroom hamper.

"How did you ever survive it?" Molly asked.

Easy, Janey thought. I took one look at the lay of the land and chose the coward's way out. A rueful twist to her lips, Janey recalled, "I dropped out of college and stayed in Colorado."

"Just like that?"

Janey gestured to indicate her regret. "I was pretty impulsive." And occasionally still was. Otherwise, she never would have made love with Thad the other night. Fortunately, these days, the demands of motherhood and the need to set a good example for her son kept her on the straight and narrow 99.9 percent of the time. At least that had been the case before she had fallen hard and fast for Thad Lantz.

Intuiting the direction of Janey's thoughts, Molly

said, "I'm so glad you and Thad are getting together."

"This is our first date," Janey sputtered self-consciously.

"So?" The smile on Molly's lips finally reached her eyes. "I saw the way he looked at you when you two walked in together tonight. You probably never met Renee—"

Janey shook her head.

"Well, suffice it to say he never looked at Renee that way, even when they were first getting together." Molly went to the mirrored dressing table and sat down in front of it. She took a small brush from her evening bag and ran it through her hair, restoring order to the dark, naturally curly strands. "Her son, Bobby, was another matter. Thad was always crazy about Bobby. So much so that he was totally destroyed when the marriage broke up and he had to relinquish custody rights. But I guess he told you about all that?"

"We've talked about it a little," Janey allowed uneasily, telling herself there were actually no parallels from Thad's past to the current situation. Yes, Thad liked Chris. But it was his interest in her, that had him coming around that often, making sure they had daily reasons to see each other. Not to mention looking at her as if she were the only woman on earth for him and kissing her at every single opportunity....

"Well, anyway," Molly continued, "Thad's always wanted a family of his own and I know he still wants to be a dad. So that makes it good for you, too.

Instead of Christopher being a detriment to any romance you might have with Thad, the fact you have a son is actually kind of a key selling point, you know?''

Janey had never thought of it that way.

Until now, anyway.

''WHATEVER YOU SAID to my sister really calmed her down,'' Thad noted as Janey found Thad talking to his father moments later, while a smiling Molly went off to find Johnny.

And totally unnerved me, Janey thought, still reeling a little from the notion that a big part of Thad's attraction to her might be her son. The fact that she came with a ready-made family.

With difficulty, Janey turned her thoughts back to the bride. ''I think Molly's going to be okay,'' Janey told both men. ''She's just nervous and a little emotional.'' And possibly—like Janey herself at that point after her own marriage—was already regretting her impulsive decision but didn't know quite what to do about it without sacrificing every ounce of pride she had in the bargain.

''I'm glad to hear it,'' Thad's father, Gordon Lantz, said. He was, like Janey's own mother, in his early fifties. The years had been kind to him—perhaps because the owner of the most popular garden and landscape center in the area had a job that kept him working outdoors year round, as well as physically fit. His tall, lean physique was every bit as handsome and distinguished as his suntanned features and neat, graying hair.

Gordon smiled at Janey. "How are those broccoli plants I gave you working out?"

"So far, so good." Although she hadn't known Thad growing up, she had been acquainted with his father for years, and felt very comfortable with the warm, personable man. "But since it's my first year trying to grow a vegetable garden on my own I'm not going to brag about it until I actually get a crop of everything I set out this spring."

"That's right," Gordon recollected kindly. "You didn't garden in Colorado, did you?"

Janey shook her head. "The growing season was too short. And I didn't really have the time or space." She hadn't owned her own home there. She, Chris and Ty had always lived in apartments because Ty hadn't wanted to be tied down. Which was why when she had moved back to Holly Springs, she had resolved to rent a house with a yard, with an option to buy when her finances improved to the point she could manage a down payment on a mortgage and closing costs. She'd thought it would be better for Chris.

The waiters came out, bearing trays of champagne and sparkling cider. Thad's stepfather came over to collect Thad for the toasts. "Show-time!" The two men headed for the raised platform at the other end of the ballroom where the DJ for the evening had set up.

As both fathers spoke of their hopes for the marriage, Molly and Johnny stood side by side. Janey didn't know if it was just the spotlight and the scrutiny being heaped upon them, but both had the look of deer caught in the headlights. To loosen them up, perhaps, Johnny's dad turned to him. "Maybe you'd like to say a few words to your bride, about your own hopes for the future?" Ted Byrne asked.

Johnny looked as if he'd rather sing karaoke, and Johnny didn't sing. He turned to Molly, posture stiff as a board. "Three years ago, when we first started dating, I never imagined we'd be standing here today as man and wife, but here we are," he said with forced cheer. "And I know in my heart—I'll always know—it was the right thing to do," he finished soberly.

For the first time since the toasts began, Molly's plastered-on smile began to slip precariously.

"Molly," her dad prompted, hoping—like everyone else assembled in the ballroom—that she would be able to save the rather odd turn the moment had taken. Dutifully, Molly took Johnny's hand in hers and looked into his eyes. "When you married me last weekend, I got what I had wished for a very long time," she said, her voice trembling audibly. "I want to thank you for that—because your willingness to stand up with me tells me what kind of man you are and always will be."

"What about love?" someone behind Janey whispered.

What indeed? Janey wondered. Thus far, the only ones who had spoken of love were the two fathers.

The DJ hired to MC the event stepped forward, glass raised. He seemed to know that to let the toasts go on any longer would be to court disaster. "To the bride and groom!" the DJ stated with the enthusiasm his job required. "And the happily-ever-after they deserve!"

"Here, here." The murmur rippled through the crowd, as crystal clinked, and congratulatory sips were taken.

Up on the bandstand platform, Thad kissed his sister, shook Johnny's hand, then wound his way back to Janey's side. "Well, that was interesting," he murmured as the music started up again.

No kidding, Janey thought, as Thad pulled her into his arms and they swayed gently to the romantic ballad. She'd never heard such odd toasts, and having grown up and worked many a wedding on The Wedding Inn ground, she thought she had just about heard it all by now. But seeking for a way to reassure Thad, she theorized practically, "They just weren't prepared to speak in front of such a large group." There had to be two hundred people assembled there that evening.

"I hope that's all it is," Thad frowned, cutting his sister a protective glance as she danced.

"I CAN'T BELIEVE you've never done this before!" Thad teased Janey a little while later as they tied the string of cans to the bumper and put the Just Married sign in the back window of the Bentley.

"Never any reason." Janey straightened, glad to finally be alone with him. "It's sort of a guy thing."

"So is this," Thad murmured in a low, sexy voice as he took her into his arms.

Janey tipped her face to his. Her heart was beating double-time. Lower still, there was a warm, fluttery feeling. "What?" she asked, ignoring the tingling in her breasts and the hard implacable ridge of his own arousal.

Thad grinned, capturing the hands she had pressed across his chest. "Kissing your woman."

His woman, Janey thought, as his mouth came down on hers. Was that what she was to him?

It certainly felt that way as his mouth moved beneath her jaw, down her throat, then back up again, to her lips. Janey couldn't help it—she moaned, and then his lips were pressed firmly on hers, just the way she had wanted them to be all night long. His tongue dipped into her mouth, stroking the insides, tangling with her tongue. Janey made a helpless sound in the back of her throat, and went up on tiptoe, meeting him caress for caress. She burned like fire. And it was a fire only he could put out. She was trembling fiercely when he let her go. Wanting...so much more.

"I wish we didn't have to go back inside," she said, not caring that she was once again putting her heart and soul on the line.

Thad's eyes darkened ardently as he tenderly locked gazes with her. "So do I," he murmured sincerely as he bent his head to kiss her again. Sweetly, this time, thoroughly. And that was when they heard the discreet feminine cough.

Janey and Thad broke apart, and turned. Helen Hart was standing there, a wicker basket of organza and ribbon-wrapped bundles of birdseed in hand. She looked both stunned and irritated by what she had seen. "I thought I'd let you know Molly and Johnny are about ready to leave for their honeymoon," Helen said politely. "People will be coming out shortly. I was hoping I could get you to pass these out for me." Helen looked at Janey meaningfully.

Janey knew that look. It meant two things. One—break it up, before anyone else witnessed the public display of affection. And two, she and her mother were going to have "a talk" the first chance Helen got.

"Not too happy about catching us kissing, was she?" Thad murmured, not quite sure what to make of Janey's mother's reaction, as Helen headed back inside the Inn.

Trying to feel thirty-three instead of oh—thirteen—Janey linked her arm through Thad's as they ascended the semicircular staircase that led to the grand covered portico that comprised the entrance to the century-old inn.

"She just worries about me," Janey explained as diplomatically as possible as they stepped inside the marble-floored foyer.

Helen didn't want to see Janey hurt again, any more than Janey wanted to be disappointed by getting too quickly—and too passionately—involved with the wrong man.

"JANEY, MAY I HAVE a word with you?"

Ah, darn. She had been hoping to avoid this until morning, at the very least. Trying her best to disguise the tension in her slender frame, Janey continued folding the box that would hold the top of the wedding cake—which would be frozen and eaten in celebration of Molly and Johnny Byrne's first anniversary as tradition dictated. She smiled at her mother as if she didn't know what was coming. "Really nice reception, Mom."

"Thank you. I thought so, too." Helen stepped nearer as the Inn's wait staff cleared tables and the DJ carted out his sound equipment. At the far end of the grand ballroom, the Byrne family and Molly's parents were loading stacks of unopened wedding presents onto carts for transport home to await the newlyweds' return from their four-day honeymoon in Bermuda. "I didn't know you were actually dating Thad Lantz," her mother continued in the same way-too-casual tone.

I am far too old for this, Janey thought, resenting the third degree. "You mean you thought I was just kissing him?" Janey asked sweetly, subtly warning her mother this was a path they did not want to take.

Helen raised a brow, even as Janey wished—too late—she could take back the prickly note in her voice and the defensiveness in her attitude. Janey didn't know why—Helen got along famously with all five of her sons—but this mother-daughter-conflict-thing was something they hadn't quite worked out of their relationship. Janey wished her mother would trust her a little more in the romance department. Not that, Janey admitted ruefully to herself, she had yet ever done anything to deserve said confidence. Before Ty, she'd had a string of rebels without a cause and various other losers to her credit. To the point her brothers had teased her about being a "bum magnet." But her relationship with Thad Lantz felt different. It felt real, and grown-up and genuine in a way no other romance ever had. It felt as if she and Thad could actually have something lasting.

Helen continued regarding Janey soberly. "I just— I wouldn't want to see this end badly," she concluded finally.

Janey's self-confidence eroded inevitably once again. "And you think it will," she retorted as she slid the cake top onto the small crystal serving platter.

"What I know is that Thad hasn't been serious about anyone for long since his divorce from Renee. His mother is a friend of mine and Veronica's said many a time that Thad never got over losing his stepson, Bobby."

"So I heard." Janey was really beginning to get irritated now. As if she didn't have enough doubts and misgivings all on her own.

As Janey slid the protective freezer wrap over the cake, Helen continued, more gently now. "I know Chris adores him. He talks about him all the time when he is with me."

To me, too, Janey affirmed, aware that up until now she had figured that was a good thing.

"If you didn't have a son, I would say let the chips fall where they may." Helen reached over to assist as Janey put the cake in the gift box. "But you do, and he could get hurt here, too."

"So what are you suggesting, Mom?" Janey closed the top of the box and regarded her mother impatiently. "That I sneak around and hide behind corners?"

Helen watched Janey tie a white satin ribbon around the box top, to ensure it stayed closed. "All I am suggesting is that you slow it down. Get to know him first, as a friend."

Good thing her mother didn't know she had already made love with Thad, even before their first date, Janey thought guiltily as she picked up the gift box.

"Everything okay here?" Thad asked amiably as he came up to join them.

Helen exuded the steel-magnolia smile she gave all Janey's potential suitors from the time Janey was old enough to date. "I was just advising my daughter not to wear her heart on her sleeve," Helen retorted gently as she looked Thad straight in the eye, the warning on her face unmistakable. "Don't let her feisty exterior fool you. My daughter has one of the most vulnerable hearts around."

THEY TOOK A SHORTCUT through the formal gardens to the far side of the parking lot, where Thad's SUV was located.

Once they were alone, Thad touched Janey playfully on the nose, not the least bit intimidated by the genteel-voiced cautioning. "Your mom's tough, huh?"

"Oh, yeah." Janey sighed. "When it comes to her brood of six, my mother doesn't mess around." And that left Janey feeling oddly protected, even as she resented her mother's interference in her blossoming love life.

Thad grinned, his ardent glance roving her up-turned face. "Well now I see where you get it," he murmured as he took her hand in his and squeezed it tightly.

Feeling comforted by his touch, Janey wrinkled her nose at him. "What do you mean?"

Thad paused in the shadow of the roses. The sweet fragrance of the flowers surrounded them. He looked down at her tenderly. "You're the same way with Chris. You think anyone is hurting or misleading him—or even has the capacity to do it—and watch out!"

Janey flushed self-consciously as she dug the toe of her evening sandal into the brick path beneath them. The skirt of her chantilly lace dress swished softly around her thighs as she moved. "Well, I don't know why she thinks you would hurt me."

Thad tucked a hand beneath her chin, and lifted her face to his. "Maybe she sees the way you look at me when you think no one is looking."

Janey flushed all the more, warming everywhere his glance touched, and everywhere it hadn't. "I don't—"

"Yes," Thad murmured, heedlessly ignoring the warning they had just received from her mother and taking her into his arms once again, "you do." He tunneled his hands through her hair, burying his fingers in the thick chestnut silk. "But that doesn't explain why your entire family seems to think you can't be trusted to make the right decisions about much of anything on your own."

Afraid they would start kissing again if they stood that way much longer, Janey took Thad's hand and led him over to one of the stone benches that lined the path. "You noticed, hmm?" she said as she sat down, urging him to do the same.

Thad nodded as he settled beside her.

Janey turned so their knees were touching. "I'm afraid it goes back to my youth."

Thad covered their clasped hands with his other palm. His eyes connected with hers and held. "What did you do—besides elope with someone you barely knew—that was so wrong?"

Trying not to think how much she liked the tantalizing scent of his aftershave, Janey shrugged and avoided his penetrating gaze. "Oh, a little bit of everything," she sighed, turning her attention to the full moon shining down upon them. "There was the time when I was fifteen when I got it into my head that I should cut my waist-length hair to a mere inch and dye it the most godawful color of red you ever saw. I cried for days when I saw the results," she recollected with a bantering smile meant to disguise the way she felt.

"And then there was the time I accidentally dented my brother Cal's car and decided to fix it myself with putty and paint, so I wouldn't have to tell anyone what I'd done. Needless to say after I was done with it, the repairs ended up costing twice as much. Or there was the time when I was a senior in high school and I overslept and missed the bus, so I decided to drive myself to the marching band competition in Virginia and got hopelessly lost in the mountains and ran out of gas. I was grounded for three months for that one."

A teasing grin curved the corners of his lips. "You were a little wild, weren't you?"

"Until I got pregnant with Chris." She swallowed around the sudden tightness in her throat, rose as gracefully as she had seated herself. "Since then, I've made a concerted effort to look before I leap," she told him firmly as they continued down the path to the cars.

Thad wrapped a comforting arm about her shoulders. "To the point you've forgotten how to take chances?"

Janey whirled to face him. Unable to ignore the bait, she defended herself hotly, "I still take chances. I moved back here. I started my own business." If that wasn't taking risks, she didn't know what was.

Thad said tenderly, "You know what I mean."

Yes, she did. "I took a chance with you, too."

The way he looked at her then, she knew he was thinking about the wonderful way they had made love. And that he wanted to do it again every bit as much as she did.

Unlike her, he did not seem to have any reservations about doing so.

"I know you did," he said gently, scoring his thumb across her lips, before continuing in a voice that melted her resistance. "And, just so you know? The first chance we get, I'm going to show you why you did."

Chapter Eight

Janey woke Saturday morning buoyant with the knowledge that Thad fully intended to make love to her again the first chance he got. That carried her through the busy morning and afternoon as she finished and delivered four more wedding and groom cakes to the appropriate Raleigh and Chapel Hill hotels. She returned home around five to find Chris grinning from ear to ear.

"What's up with you?" Janey asked curiously, as she set the mail down on the kitchen table. He looked as happy as if he'd just been drafted to the NHL.

"My summer school teacher, Ms. Havelock, called and came by with my papers and unit tests. She said she didn't think I should have to wait until I came back from hockey camp to see them." He thrust them at Janey proudly.

Janey looked down at the papers. There were red A's slashed across the top of every single homework paper, and an A-plus on his unit tests for five and six.

"Wow," Janey said, stunned. She was used to seeing A's on Chris's other work. Never his math. In math, he always seemed to struggle just to get a passing grade. She looked at her son, so proud of his accomplishment she could burst. "This is wonderful, Chris." She hugged him fiercely.

"So can I go celebrate?" Chris asked.

Janey set down her car keys and shoulder bag. She cast an eye at the answering machine. No messages, she noted with disappointment. "Where do you want to go?"

"Out with my friends. There's the new *Star Wars* movie playing in Raleigh, at the megaplex, and Tommy's dad said he would take all of us to the movie and then out to get pizza and play video games. The thing is, we won't be back 'til real late, like between midnight and one on account of he has to drop all six of us off one by one."

It sounded like quite an evening. "You realize you have to go to hockey camp tomorrow."

"I'm all packed already." Chris pointed to the gear stacked neatly in the corner of the living room. "And sign-in isn't until three."

Given how hard he had been working, Chris deserved the reward, Janey knew. "Okay. You need some money?" She took out her billfold.

"Nope." Chris pulled a twenty out of his pocket. "Coach Lantz paid me for working this week, so I can use this for tonight and apply the rest—' Janey watched as Chris pulled several other bills out of his pocket "—toward my camp fees if that is all right with you."

PROUD OF THE WAY her son was handling his new-found responsibility, Janey waved goodbye to Chris and his friends as Tommy's dad backed his van out of the driveway.

Smiling to herself, Janey went upstairs and ran herself a bubble bath. Stripping off her clothes, she sank into it, and thought about what she might wear that evening should Thad call and ask to see her.

She was still deciding when she got out of the tub.

Concluding it was silly to even think about it, since she didn't know where she was going—or even if she was going out at all—she wrapped the robe around herself.

Padding barefoot back down to the kitchen, she fixed herself a cup of tea and contemplated going ahead and having something for dinner. As she was looking over the contents of the fridge, she realized this was the part of dating—and even married life—that she had always hated. The waiting around for a phone call. Wanting to see someone. Not knowing if they wanted or intended to see you.

Janey sighed. This was ridiculous. She was an adult. If she wanted to see him, she would simply go and see him.

DROPPING BY WITHOUT WARNING seemed like a great idea—less pressure—and was confirmed when Janey drove up in front of Thad's home and saw his SUV in the driveway. Already rehearsing her thoroughly planned opening banter, she got out of the car, went to the front door and rang the bell. Or tried. It didn't take her long to realize the bell wasn't ringing.

Fortunately, she could hear the sound of music emanating from the backyard. Her pulse racing in anticipation of seeing him again, Janey started around the side of the house. The gate was unlocked and, feeling only a tad awkward, she walked on through it. Beginning to be a little nervous now—what if it was a bad time, or he wasn't so keen on seeing her after all—she closed the gate in the privacy fence behind her and continued a little less certainly around the landscaped flowers and miniature shrubbery that stretched from the fence to the deck.

Telling herself that since she was here now she might as well make the best of it, she started up the steps, her most cheerful smile on her face.

And that was when she realized two things simultaneously. The up-tempo music—suitable for a twenty-something dance club—was not at all Thad's normal style. Not as Janey knew it anyway. And two, he wasn't as alone as she thought.

Through the bank of kitchen windows that stretched the length of the deck, Janey could see the man who had secretly stolen her heart. He was standing in front of the stainless steel stove, tending something in a pot. A beautiful blonde, a good ten years his junior, was dancing around Thad in what was a definite come-on. She was accentuating her moves with the wooden spoon in her hand.

Thad was obviously trying not to smile as she con-

tinued her sinuous belly dance, but lost the battle as
her moves became more and more outrageous.

Soon, both were laughing uproariously.

And all the while, Janey just stood there, staring,
unable to move, unable to comprehend what she was
seeing. Thad had another girlfriend? A younger girlfriend?

Suddenly, all Janey wanted to do was get out of
there, go home and lick her wounds. She had headed
back down the half-dozen steps of the deck and
landed on the grass when Thad turned in her direction. Figuring the way she had just humiliated herself
was enough, without him knowing about it, too, Janey
ducked down out of sight. Only to have him open the
French doors leading out to the deck.

Janey had two choices. Stand and be recognized
then and there. Or hope he hadn't caught sight of her,
and get down, under the two-and-a-half-feet-high
deck and hide out until she could make a swift unseen
getaway. She chose the latter.

"Okay, Thad," Janey heard the blonde say as the
feet moved overtop of where she was crouched.
"Now you really *really* have to look as if you're enjoying yourself."

"Oh, I am," Thad enthused as he moved something around above her. Looking up, Janey noticed it
was the gas grill.

Crouching on her hands and knees, she moved well
to the left of the two pairs of feet moving around above
her. She could only hope he didn't look down and

see the flash of color of her clothes between the slats. Why hadn't she worn something less...vibrant?

The young beauty giggled. "I'm serious, Coach. You look like such a grouch."

Thad harrumphed. "Maybe because I was told this wasn't going to take long at all."

"Oh, now, just calm down and open up the first couple of buttons on your shirt. Alicia—are you ready to go too?"

There was another woman? Janey thought, stunned. What exactly was going on here?

More footsteps sounded on the deck. Judging by the weight of the steps—and the perfume scenting the air—Alicia was another young beauty. "I think she's right about the shirt," Alicia said in a sexy rumble. "Because we want you to look really hot."

Was this how Thad got his kicks? Was he kinkier in his private life than she ever could have imagined?

"I am hot," Thad complained in a deep sexy voice that sent tremors of awareness shooting through Janey.

The first young beauty giggled appreciatively at Thad's grumpily voiced quip. "Oh, Coach. Not that kind of hot!"

Janey knew what Thad meant. She had only been crouched in the July heat for five minutes and she was already sweating. Getting bit by about a thousand mosquitoes, too, if the itching of her skin beneath her short white denim skirt and turquoise blue T-shirt were any indication.

"Okay, I've got the wieners!" yet another female voice said. "Where do you want 'em?"

And sure enough, now that she took a good whiff, Janey *did* smell hot dogs cooking. She didn't know whether she was relieved or irritated that Thad was now surrounded by a bevy of females.

"On the grill," Thad directed, obviously as exasperated as Janey was beginning to be confused.

"And you need an apron."

"Yeah! One that says Kiss the Chef!"

"Oh, now you look cute." Feet moved as the beauties moved back to survey him, just so.

"Doesn't he?"

"Just take the picture and get it over with!" Thad growled.

"Oh, Coach," the first young woman giggled uproariously again, "We're going to need a lot more than one good view of you before any of us will be satisfied!"

THAD WAS TRYING, but this was not his cup of tea. Still, it was for charity, he forced himself to remember as the twenty-two-year-old wife of one of the senior players on the team and an equally young and silly female photographer and two other wives put him through two dozen poses and numerous shots of him manning the grill, until finally even *they'd* had enough.

"You've been such a good sport." Alanna Morgan bussed his cheek with the southern familiarity that passed as both hello and goodbye.

"And we do appreciate your patience," the other two wives agreed.

He wasn't all that patient, Thad thought, as he rushed them through the house as politely as possible and out the front door. And that was when he saw the Delectable Cakes bakery delivery minivan parked on the street in front of his house. He waited until the women had driven off in the limo that came to collect them and all their equipment, then went over to the vehicle. It was locked. Janey was not inside. Which was odd, Thad thought, because he didn't see her anywhere in his front yard, or on the street of luxury homes, either. So she couldn't have been there to make a delivery. Could she?

Puzzled, he started back across the yard, toward the front door, and that was when he decided to check one more thing and noticed the latch on the privacy fence was ajar. And suddenly he had an idea where Janey might be.

Smiling, he pushed open the gate, strode around the side of the house, and—unbelievably—saw a tell-tale flash of turquoise blue and white behind the flowers and miniature shrubbery that surrounded the base of the deck.

"Should I close my eyes and count backwards from ten?" he wondered sardonically out loud. "Or just say 'Come out, come out, wherever you are'?"

JANEY SWORE furiously.

"If you don't come out of there right now," Thad warned, "I'm coming in right after you."

"I think I'll just stay right where I am, thank you very much," Janey retorted stiffly, wondering if it was possible to be any more humiliated than she already was. Somehow, she didn't think so.

To her dismay, Thad hunkered down so she could see him—and he could see her, hunched over in the filthy mixture of pine straw and red Carolina mud beneath the wooden deck. "Okay." He rubbed his hands together as if he couldn't relish the prospect any more. "Coming in!"

Janey didn't think he would really do it, but he did. Before she could do more than draw a quick breath or two, he had slid beneath the decking and crouched down next to her on his knees. "Kind of like being in a grade-school clubhouse, isn't it?" He looked around admiringly before focusing in with disturbing intensity on her flushed face. "Except this one is a lot better made than anything I ever put together with a hammer and nails."

So furious over what she had seen and heard, it was all Janey could do not to smack the smug smile off his handsome face. "Handy, were you?" she drawled as she sat back on her heels, figuring if he could breeze his way through this, so could she.

"Oh, yeah. I am now, too," he boasted sexily. "But then I guess you saw that."

"Sort of," she replied, determined to give nothing of what she knew away while she waited to see how much he would confess to. Then she pressed her lips together in a sick parody of a smile. "The view from down here isn't that good."

"I see what you mean." Thad glanced upward before reaching over and putting both palms on her bare knees. He leaned forward urgently, so they were face to face and nose to nose. "Which begs the question—why are you down here?"

Janey began to flush. Unfortunately, given the way her weight was distributed over her legs from ankle to knee, she couldn't move backward with any degree of gracefulness. So once again, she remained where she was, pretending as if she did things this ludicrous every single day. "I stopped by," she answered him with feigned mildness.

Looking mouthwateringly attractive in a black silk Hawaiian print shirt, olive green shorts, and deck shoes, he arched a dark brow. "Beneath my deck?" he repeated drolly.

Janey shrugged, aware her lower legs were beginning to ache from the awkward position. "Your doorbell doesn't work."

"Well that certainly explains it."

"I heard music." Feeling more foolish by the second, Janey gestured inanely. "I came around to say hello, and saw you dancing or being danced around by the cute little blonde, got worried I was interrupting a tête-à-tête of some sort and—"

He looked abruptly pleased in the way men looked when the woman in their life became jealous. "Panicked?" Thad guessed.

Janey shrugged, refusing to admit to anything more at this point. She returned his reproving look with a saccharine one of her own. "Well, I guess I could say

I dropped an earring and came beneath here to find it," she said sarcastically, "but I doubt you would believe it."

"No kidding." He didn't do much to curtail an amused smirk. His voice dropped a compelling notch as he leaned forward to whisper in her ear, his warm minty breath ghosting over her face, "Especially since you're not wearing earrings, and don't seem to have any in your possession, either."

"So, anyway," Janey removed his palms from her knees. She no longer cared as much about maintaining her dignity as much as ending the sensual tension simmering between them. Pulse racing, she scrambled away from him. "Now that we've said hello," she said, scraping her knees in the muddy pine straw, "I guess I'll be going." Clearing the deck on all fours, she tried not to think about what a ridiculously disheveled sight she must be as she stumbled to her feet. All she wanted to do was get out of there, but no, Thad came out after her and caught her hand before she could escape.

Standing, he leisurely surveyed her muddy, itchy body. "When you arrived, did you by any chance have welts breaking out on your arms and legs?"

"No." Janey pulled the hem of her T-shirt back down over her belly button. "But then," she said, smacking ineffectually at her arm, and then her leg, wondering just what it was she had been kneeling in. Some sort of nest? "I wasn't itching then, either."

"Then I say we get you out of here—" he knocked

a blood-sucking insect off her shoulder ''—before the mosquitoes eat us both alive.''

THAD CHIVALROUSLY HELPED HER up onto the deck and led the way into the kitchen. ''I don't know what you think was going on here tonight,'' he started casually.

Janey pushed the suspicious thoughts from her mind. Fair or not, she couldn't bear to think of him with another woman. Or women. ''I'm not sure I need to know,'' she told him stiffly, turning away from him.

He, however, thought she did. Clamping his hands on her shoulders, he brought her right back around. ''The wives of the players were here to work on the cookbook for charity. The one your brother Joe and his wife Emma are also participating in,'' he said, jogging her memory politely.

''Oh,'' Janey said. *No*…

''Now that my part in it is done, is there anything else you would like to ask me?'' he asked.

Feeling like more of a fool than ever, Janey swallowed. If ever a change of subject was in order it's now, she thought as she rubbed at a swelling welt on her shin. ''How come I got bit by what looks like a thousand insects just now and you didn't?'' As far as she could see, he didn't have a single bite on him— and very little mud—since he had simply hunkered down and rested his weight on his deck-shoe-clad feet.

''It's probably your perfume.'' His gaze drifted

over her rumpled turquoise T-shirt and twisted-around white skirt. "You smell...incredible—to the bugs, as well as me!" He grinned at her, teasing now, as his hands ghosted over her spine to her shoulders, down her arms. "Want to sit down?" he asked.

Janey looked at his nice furniture and her smudged clothing and despite her fervent wish he would haul her into his arms and kiss her, said, "I'm not sure I should."

"Yeah," Thad agreed with her unexpectedly, "you are a mess." He rubbed at her cheek with the pad of his thumb. When he took it away, it was covered with dirt.

"Oh, man," Janey lamented emotionally, scratching all the harder, her humiliation complete.

"You know, I hate to say it," Thad continued candidly, already guiding her toward the stairs off the kitchen, "but I think you need to get into the shower ASAP, and get some soap and water on those insect bites. And while you're doing that, I'll make us some dinner."

Janey took a wild guess. "Hot dogs?"

"Don't make fun." He regarded her with mock censure. "They're a sports fan's delight."

He propelled her down a long carpeted hall, toward the master bedroom. It was beautifully appointed, masculine. With heavy mahogany furniture, custom bronze and black bed linens and curtains. The bathroom was equally beautiful—with tan ceramic tile, white cabinetry, black marble countertops, Jacuzzi tub and shower. "Toss your clothes out, and I'll put them in the wash."

"And then what?" Janey asked uncertainly, aware he was sending her more than a few mixed messages. "I wait in here until my clothes are dry?"

"No, silly, you put on my robe and come down to the kitchen where I'll have a glass of wine waiting for you." He paused. "Unless of course you want to go home looking like you've been rolling around in my backyard?"

"Very funny." Unfortunately, he was right. Her neighbors liked to walk their dogs, ride their bikes and sit on front porches this time of evening. If she left his place looking like this, there would be questions that might even make their way back to her mother. That was the last thing she needed. "All right. I accept your offer," Janey said reluctantly. "But I'm counting on you to be a gentleman."

His eyes gleamed. "I promise I'll be as good to you as I know how to be," he said in a low voice dripping with innuendo.

Janey shook her head, but didn't deny the thought of making love with him again was incredibly tempting.

Smiling, he stepped outside the bathroom and turned his back.

Janey stripped off her clothes, including the sheer white demi-bra and matching thong panties, and tossed them at him through the narrow opening in the slightly ajar bathroom door. He chuckled as he caught them but did not turn around before setting off in the opposite direction. Marvelling at his willpower—she wasn't sure if she would have been able to resist putting the moves on him if the situation had been reversed—she closed the door completely, turned the water to hot and stepped beneath the massaging showerhead. Being careful not to get her hair wet, she luxuriated in the smell of the masculine fragrance of the soap he used. Secretly thrilled at the intimacy of showering where he did, she wondered what it would be like to make love in here, against the wall. If it would be as good as the first time they'd been together. She wondered if he was as hungry for her as she was for him.

Her mind laced with erotic fantasies, she could have stayed there all day. Not wanting him to come and check up on her, though—that was a little too obvious, even for her—she got out, toweled off, and slipped on his robe. It was way too big for her and smelled deliciously like him, too. She wrapped the belt around her twice, ran a brush through her hair, and went to join him in the kitchen.

To her surprise, he had prepared a plate of cheese and a large salad, and lo and behold, he did have a pan of hot dogs and another of chili simmering in a small condiment-size Crock-Pot on the counter. Janey glanced at the liquid simmering in the pan. "Is that...beer?" she asked in surprise.

"Mmm-hmm." Thad brought a bag of soft squishy buns from the pantry, and got all the hot-dog fixings from the fridge. He shot her a glance, seeming to like the way she looked in his robe. "Ever tried it?"

"I guess I'm going to," Janey allowed, as she slipped barefoot onto one of the stools at the marble-topped center island. "Is this what you were doing earlier when the other women were here?"

Thad nodded. "The secret is to simmer the franks in beer for at least twenty minutes, and then sear them on the grill. Really brings out the flavor."

Funny, she had never seen him as at all domestic. But then, there was a lot she had yet to learn about him—a lot she wanted to learn. "And you know this because?" She sipped her wine.

Thad sat down on the stool next to her, his back to the counter. "My first year coaching in the minor leagues, I also majored in hot-dog science."

Janey blinked in confusion. "Excuse me?"

Thad picked up his wine. "I was really poor because the only people who make less than the players in the minor leagues are the assistant coaches." He shrugged his broad shoulders amiably. "Hot dogs were the only thing I knew how to cook. So I cut a deal with the concessions manager at the rink where we played our games, bought a case of hot dogs for cost, and took 'em back to my apartment and put them in the freezer." The corners of his lips turned up ruefully. "You have no idea how tired you can get of hot dogs if you eat them every single day for lunch and dinner."

Janey smiled. "I think I can imagine." About as tired as she was of cake, any kind of cake.

"I mean I cooked 'em in pork and beans and in casseroles, and ate 'em plain and barbecued and with sauerkraut and onions. By the end of that first year, when I finally got a raise and could afford a steak and a chicken every now and then, I never wanted to see another hot dog.''

"And yet," Janey said softly, aware she was seeing a new side of Thad, a vulnerable side, "you are cooking them tonight."

"Because I had to—for the team cookbook. And—" his voice dropped significantly, as he searched her eyes "—'cause I like to remind myself that I come from very humble beginnings and any success I have is just as temporary as any failure."

Janey's smile widened. "That's deep," she teased, trying hard not to fall head over heels in love with him.

He winked at her flirtatiously. "And here you thought I was just a dumb son-of-a-gun who tells jocks how to push a puck around the ice." Thad patted her on the knee.

"I don't think you're dumb," Janey said as he slid off the stool, shut off the stove, and began getting out the barbecue utensils and setting them on the counter.

"You don't?"

Janey slid off her stool and went to stand next to him. "A dumb guy couldn't have gotten me out of my clothes and into his shower within the first fifteen minutes of my arrival here tonight."

Thad grinned as he leaned back against the counter, folded his arms and gave her the sexy once-over.

"You do look rather nice in my robe," he allowed in a low, sultry tone.

"And," Janey said recklessly, opening it up and letting it fall to the floor. "I look even better without it."

Chapter Nine

Thad had been prepared to do a lot more persuading, but that mission was proved unnecessary when Janey closed the distance between them and wrapped her arms snugly around him. She rose up on tiptoe, the softness of her breasts pressing against his chest, the soapy clean scent of her skin inundating his senses. "I think," she whispered against his lips, her yearning for him as clear as day, "this is the part where you kiss me again."

It was always the sweet and seemingly unattainable ones that turned out to be the most uninhibited, Thad thought, as her mouth opened beneath his and their tongues mated in an erotic dance like nothing he had ever imagined. And Janey Hart Campbell was one wild and feisty woman.

Pleasure swept through him and he continued kissing her as he stepped between her legs. Anchoring an arm beneath her softly curving derrière, he lifted her up and situated Janey so her weight was settled against his middle. As a mischievously grinning Janey wreathed her arms about his neck and wrapped her legs around his waist, Thad felt his spirits soar even more. He didn't know why or how he had been given this gift. He didn't care. He only knew he was never letting this sweet and sexy woman go.

"This time we're doing it right," he murmured as he carried her up the stairs, loving the way she felt so soft and naked and warm against him. "We're going to my bed."

"How...tame..." she teased him between hot, openmouthed kisses, stroking a hand down his chest and sliding it beneath the open neck of his shirt.

"Believe me—there's nothing tame about what I want to do to you," he said as he tumbled her down onto his king-sized bed, enjoying the sight of her with her cheeks all flushed, her silky chestnut hair spilling over her shoulders, her body already visibly ready for him.

Janey reclined on her side, curves displayed sexily for his perusal and watched him undress. He knew what she presumed as she struggled to keep this on a strictly playful level—that this was just about sex. But it wasn't, he thought, as he joined her on the bed and stretched out facing her. It was so very much more— their hearts and minds and souls had been engaged from the very first. "I've been thinking about this since that first time...."

He trailed a hand over the indentation of her waist, the curve of her hip, the lissome line of her thigh, watching as her lips parted softly. Her breath was coming in soft fits and starts as she watched him caress her abdomen.

"So have I."

She looked so full of need for him, it nearly stopped his heart. Pulse pounding, senses already in an uproar, he cupped his hand over the bare flesh of her buttocks and squeezed gently. It was going to be a hell of an effort, but this time, he promised himself, he was going to go slow. Make sure she got every ounce of enjoyment out of this, and then some.

"About all the things I didn't do," Thad continued lazily as his palm inched upward, toward her breasts. "And want to do."

She hitched in a breath as he explored the satiny pink tip of her nipple with the pad of his thumb and kissed him back pliantly. "I think you covered it pretty well," she murmured sexily.

He stroked her lovely curves, moving from the tempting roundness of one breast to the other and back again, letting her know he was as wild for her as she was for him. "Guess I'll have to show you differently, then," he murmured, putting everything he had into their kiss. Shifting her onto her back, he draped a leg over her thighs and continued caressing her, with the flat of his palm, the tips of his fingers, making his way from her breasts to collarbone to navel to thigh. Studiously avoiding the part he most wanted to touch he kissed her all the while, until she moaned a soft little helpless sound that sent his senses swimming as she opened her lips to him even more, and eventually her thighs.

Trembling with a need—and a depth of feeling—he could no longer deny, his gaze locked with hers as he grasped her by the waist and pulled her to the edge of the bed. Loving the no-holds-barred way she surrendered herself to him, he knelt on the floor in front of her and nudged her legs farther apart. She was as beautiful as he recalled and she whispered her delight as he breathed in the musky scent of her and stroked his fingers on the petal-pink softness. Allowing him full rein, she trembled with anticipation as he stroked her gently and then leaned forward to touch the damp silky-soft skin. Satisfaction unlike anything he had ever known roared through him and she gasped wildly as his tongue stroked the pearly bud hidden in the flesh, once, then again and again. Rubbing across it in straight lines, in tantalizing circles, then back and forth, again and again, until she was calling his name, arching, shaking, coming apart in his hands. His own body aching with the need to possess her, he held her until the shudders subsided, feeling the hot liquid of her desire flowing over her skin, readying her for him.

Janey had known all along the desire she felt for Thad—desire stronger than anything she'd ever experienced in her life—was something she just couldn't fight. So she had decided to stop struggling and just go with it, let them have a very physically satisfying fling. She'd thought that way she could keep her heart—and her emotions—out of it. But when he moved back up on the bed and took her in his arms once again, when he kissed her everywhere with the tenderness only a dream lover could possess, she knew much more was going on here, than she had ever wanted. The impossible was happening. She was falling head over heels in love with Thad. And those feelings only intensified as he lifted her against him and entered her with excruciating slowness, not stopping until he had filled her to capacity. Until his body stretched hers, filled hers, took command in a thoroughly male, thoroughly proprietary way like she had never been possessed before.

She moaned softly, tangling her hands in his hair, moving them over his shoulders, down his back, wanting him never to stop. And he didn't. Even as he slowed it down, to the point the pleasure was as hot and wanton as the emotions swirling around inside her, pausing, withdrawing and entering her again. And again. And again. Deeper every time. Kissing her all the while. Taking control, coaxing—then demanding—her surrender. Until she was kissing him back, more passionately than ever before, arching her back and rocking up against him, the fire of her desire fueling their pleasure. Until she thought she would die of the erotic feelings she had dreamed of but never experienced. Until she was shaking with sensation and came apart once again, knowing this time she was his—not just for now, but forever. And this time, he took them both into a sweet, hot oblivion that never seemed to end.

BUT OF COURSE, it did end, Janey thought wistfully as Thad shifted away from her. He wrapped his arms around her and brought her back against him so she was lying with her head on his chest, her leg thrown over one of his. And all her romantic imaginings and wishes were not going to make this anything but what it really was—a hot, wild, thoroughly enjoyable fling between two consenting adults.

"And here all I planned to give you tonight was dinner," he murmured tenderly against her hair.

Loving the sound of his heart beating so steady and strong in his chest, Janey forced her private worries aside and laughed softly. Luxuriating in the warmth of him, she kept her eyes shut and snuggled even closer.

Until Thad had come into her world, she had been living half a life, that of a mother, business owner and feisty young widow. But the side of her that was all woman had gone unfulfilled. It was going to be hard for her to give it up if and when he walked away.

Struggling against the uneasy feeling that she might have given away her heart far too easily again, Janey got out of bed.

"Not to worry, Coach," she teased him back in the same insouciant tone. "All your culinary efforts haven't been for naught—I could still go for something to eat."

He chuckled appreciatively, "Nothing like a woman with a healthy appetite."

For sex, as well as food? Janey wondered. She wished she hadn't left his robe downstairs, pooled on the kitchen floor. She needed some emotional distance from him. Some time to recoup that wall she had built around her heart to protect her from crushing disappointment once again.

Her heart pounding with the effort it was taking to affect an outward composure she couldn't begin to really feel, she sauntered to his closet. Peering in, she saw what she had been looking for. Two dozen dress shirts were lined up next to the suits. She slipped one off the hanger, put it on and came back out to face him. Pirouetting flirtatiously, she flashed him a smile. "Mind if I borrow this?"

IT WAS AMAZING HOW sexy Janey could look clad in nothing but one of his starched shirts, Thad thought, as he rose reluctantly from the rumpled sheets on his bed. "Blue never looked that good on me."

"I wouldn't be so sure of that. I think you look mighty fine in whatever you wear."

Then why was she distancing herself from him? Thad wondered as he dressed. Moments before when they had been making love, he'd felt as if nothing could ever come between them. But now Janey looked as if she were standing behind the counter and he were a bakery customer there to be waited on.

Maybe they did need to get something to eat, he thought as he wrapped his arm possessively around her shoulders and led her downstairs. It would give him time to figure out how to keep her in his life. And stop this from being just a fling on both their parts.

"SO HOW WAS your weekend?" Joe Hart's wife, Emma, asked Monday morning as she encountered

Thad in the hallway outside the executive offices at the Raleigh sports arena where Storm games were played. The daughter of team owner Saul Donovan, and public-relations whiz Margaret, Emma was a frequent visitor to Storm headquarters, as well as a successful wedding planner.

"Good," Thad replied. "And bad." He had been extremely disappointed when Janey had left right after dinner, claiming she had to get home before Christopher got back, because she didn't want Chris to know she had been with Thad again, lest he start making too much of their...friendship.

Friendship. Thad scowled. He and Janey had enjoyed the most mind-blowing sex he'd ever had in his life, and she called him her "friend." What was it with women these days anyway? Why didn't they want to commit anymore?

"Why was it bad?" Emma asked curiously.

Because Janey had made sure he had zero opportunity to speak to her since that night and he had no idea if Janey would even be able to work him into her busy schedule the rest of the week, while her son was conveniently away every night. Nights when the two of them could surreptitiously sleep together and awaken wrapped in each other's arms every single morning.

Thad wasn't a selfish man. But he wanted his time with Janey. He wanted the opportunity to make her his so completely and thoroughly she would never want anyone else, and he wasn't sure she was going to give it to him. And he didn't know what in blue blazes to do about that.

He looked up to find Emma still studying him with wise eyes. "If I didn't know better, Coach Lantz," she teased, "I'd say you were feeling just a tad... lovesick?"

Thad gave her an exasperated look. Leave it to Emma to hit the nail on the head. If only Janey could see things his way. He was about to ask if Emma had seen or talked to Janey when he caught a glimpse of a woman in a long hooded red rain cape, a big wicker basket slung over her arm. She paused just outside the door to the executive offices and pushed the hood away from her face. Thad saw a spill of rich chestnut hair and a very beautiful albeit familiar profile before the woman disappeared through the doors.

"IF YOU DON'T HAVE an appointment, there is no way you're getting in to see Saul Donovan," the secretary told Janey firmly.

Janey had been determined to achieve the business milestone completely by herself, without putting anyone on the spot or setting herself up to later be accused of only getting the gig because of social or familial ties. But as she stared failure in the face, she began to regret her decision not to presume on her friendships with Thad Lantz and/or her sister-in-law Emma, to get in to see Emma's father.

"What about the general manager, then?" Janey asked.

The secretary's smile tightened relentlessly. "He's

in with Mr. Donovan and he's not coming out, either.''

"Then when can I get an appointment?" Janey asked, beginning to feel thoroughly exasperated as well as downright wet from trudging here through the pouring rain. She had left half a dozen messages for the person responsible for making the appointments. Her calls had never been returned, or put through.

"You can't. Not if your name isn't on the list. I thought I explained that to you on the phone."

Janey leaned forward urgently. "And I explained to you that I only need five minutes of Mr. Donovan's time."

"Tough. I'm surprised the security guards let you in."

Janey wasn't. She'd flashed her sexiest smile, fibbed about having a birthday surprise for Saul from the Delectable Cakes bakery, and bribed them with some cupcakes she just happened to have with her.

"Now if you don't leave nicely I will have security come back and escort you out," the secretary told her with a look that brooked no disobedience as the door opened and shut behind Janey.

"Problem?" a familiar voice said.

Janey turned. Thad was standing there. He was wearing a knit red-and-gray shirt with Storm insignia, jeans and running shoes, appearing as fit as any member on the hockey team and equally determined to succeed. Blue eyes alight with curiosity, he looked from her to the basket in her arms, then back to her face. She was close enough to inhale the spicy scent of his cologne. Close enough to see the speculation on his face, as well as the disappointment he still obviously harbored for her refusal to sleep with him again the previous evening. "What's going on?" he demanded brusquely.

The secretary leveled an accusing finger Janey's way. "She wants to see Mr. Donovan and she does not have an appointment."

Thad folded his arms across his chest and looked into Janey's eyes, his attitude one of utter male supremacy. Neglecting to voice the questions he obviously had for Janey, he turned glibly back to the secretary. "That's easy enough to fix." He walked past her desk and on into Saul's office. Seconds later, the door opened and Saul Donovan came out. He smiled at Janey and motioned her forward. "Come on in."

JANEY PRACTICALLY SAILED down the hall as she left the executive offices, the nearly empty basket still tucked over her arm. She hadn't been this happy professionally in…well, she couldn't recall when!

She was halfway to the escalator when the familiar figure stepped out of one of the doors that led to the luxury boxes. "Hey, Red Riding Hood," he drawled. Taking her by the arm, he tugged her toward him and into the luxury box. "You sure are looking sexy today."

Janey caught her breath as Thad shut the door behind them, leaving them quite alone. "Thad!"

"Good," he said in a cool deliberate tone. "You remember my name. That's always nice."

Obviously, he was referring to the fact she had been too "busy," to see him the previous day. Janey swallowed hard. Experience had taught her that any time alone with Thad usually led to a few hot kisses, if not more. She could not afford to indulge in a sexy clinch with him, particularly here and now. "I—thank you for getting me in to see Saul."

Thad folded his arms, the action serving only to more distinctly outline the hard, masculine contours of his shoulders and chest beneath the knit shirt. "I gather whatever you were doing here was successful."

Janey smiled and tried to look suitably at ease. "Very." She paused and wet her lips. "I sold him on a business proposal. I'm going to be supplying custom-ordered birthday cakes and cupcakes to people buying birthday game packs for Storm games. And I owe it all to you for giving me the swift kick in the pants I needed to come up with the idea."

He quirked a dark brow. "I take it this means your financial problems will be subsiding, then."

Janey nodded in relief. "As soon as the legal details are worked out and I hire another pastry chef to help me at the bakery."

Thad smiled. "I'm glad to hear that."

"Well, if that's all..." Janey began to step past.

"Not so fast." He moved to block her way. "I want to know why you've been avoiding me."

"I told you." Janey drew in a steadying breath and eased back until her spine was flat against the wall. "I was working on a business proposal."

His smile flashed wickedly. "You could have made time to talk to me." He gave her a sexy once-over, then lifted his hands in an amiable fashion. "Or do you think I'm the Big Bad Wolf, now that we've made love twice?" he dared with a complacent smile.

Scowling, Janey folded her arms in front of her. She wasn't sure whether she wanted to deck him for that, or kiss him. She only knew whenever she was around him she had an overwhelming desire to make contact with him. "I wasn't aware we were counting," she said stiffly.

"Oh, we're counting all right," he drawled, still eyeing her appreciatively from head to toe, taking in the fluid lines of her gray silk jersey dress, snazzy red leather belt, and gold Carolina Storm brooch. "And I'd like to count a lot higher. The question is, Janey," Thad asked huskily, "what do you want to do?"

What *did* she want to do? Janey wondered. Did she want to continue jumping headlong into a romance with Thad, thereby risking another broken heart? Or step back a pace, and think this through? Which of course would be the logical thing to do. "Don't you have to work or something?" She brushed past him so she was no longer trapped between him and the wall. "Especially with the kids' camp going on this week?"

To her dismay, instead of taking offense at the implied criticism in her tone, he merely leaned one shoulder against the wall, and looked even more relaxed. "That's over at the practice facility, and I'll be there this afternoon." Taking one of her wrists in hand, he reeled her back into his side. "This morning, the kids are being assessed by ability and sorted into groups by the assistant coaches and the players participating, such as your brother Joe."

"Oh." Janey regarded Thad uneasily, trying without much success to wrest her forearm from the strong tantalizingly warm grip of his hand.

"I'm also free this evening when the daily scrimmages end at nine," he said, lifting her wrist to his lips and kissing the back of it lightly. "The campers will be seeing a movie at a theater in Raleigh, before being returned to the private dorm on the State campus where they are bunking."

He was doing it again, looking as if he were already making love to her. Janey cleared her throat, knowing what she said next was going to sound like a line. "I have to work."

He held her eyes with his mesmerizing gaze, making her feel all hot and bothered. "After nine?" he asked, as if he couldn't possibly have heard her right.

"Yes." She paused, then finished in her soft Carolina drawl. "Thank you for the invitation, though." If she hadn't been so determined to curtail the rapidly increasing vulnerability she felt whenever she was around him, she would have done whatever she needed to do and made the time to be with him.

He studied her a long moment, then straightened, and moved away from her. If he was unhappy with her decision, he wasn't showing it.

"Okay, then." Thad let go of her wrist and walked out.

JANEY KNEW SHE HAD no one to blame but herself for the missed supper and late hours but she had wanted to make her pitch to Saul Donovan before anyone else beat her to the punch and had let the orders for the next day's bridal shower and wedding anniversary cakes slide. Now, eight hours after saying goodbye to Thad at the arena, she was just putting the finishing touches on the last cake.

She heard a rapping on the front window and looked up to see Thad standing next to the bakery door, the expression on his face all business. Hoping nothing bad had happened to Chris—injuries were rampant in hockey, and this was another reason she didn't want her son playing—she hurried over to let Thad in. "Everything all right?" She was ridiculously glad to see him, given how up in the air they'd left things.

Thad frowned. If he found fault with her disheveled appearance, he wasn't showing it.

"Not in your son's view," Thad said, coming over to regard her handiwork with an admiring glance before turning back to face her. "He's upset you weren't there to watch the scrimmages tonight with the other parents who live in the area."

Janey took exception to his blunt tone. "I sent word through my brother Joe." She searched Thad's face, unable to help admiring how ruggedly attractive he looked with the shadow of evening beard lining his face. Like her, Thad appeared to have had a very long and arduous day. "Didn't he get my message?"

"Yes, but he thinks your absence is a sign of your

disapproval of his ambition where hockey is concerned.''

''That's ridiculous!'' Janey shot back with a toss of her head.

He caught her wrist with his free hand. ''Is it?''

Suddenly, Janey was having difficulty drawing air into her lungs. ''Definitely!''

He let her go as swiftly as he claimed her. ''Then is it me you're avoiding?''

Janey averted her gaze. ''I'm not avoiding anyone,'' she denied flatly, knowing even as she spoke it wasn't quite true. She threw up her hands. ''Why can't people understand I have to work this evening?''

Thad lifted a hand and gestured at the finished cakes. ''None of this could have been done tomorrow morning?''

Janey shook her head emphatically. ''All of these have to be delivered by noon. I've been baking since I returned from the arena at noon.''

His expression softening compassionately, Thad inclined his head at the Help Wanted sign in the window. ''How long do you think it'll take to get some extra help?'' he asked, looking ready to help with that, too, if she would let him.

''I don't know.''

Janey looked up as a second rap sounded on the storefront windows. Thad's sister Molly stood outside. She waved at the two of them and strode on in.

The first thing Janey noticed was that Molly didn't look very tan, for just having come back from a honeymoon in Bermuda. Although that could be explained...by a lot of time spent in a hotel room. The second was that Johnny wasn't with her. And that wasn't so easily explained, given the fact they were still very much newlyweds and should be glued to each other's sides.

"I saw your lights and the sign in the window and I wondered if I could apply," Molly said.

Thad interrupted with a troubled frown, "What happened to your job in Chapel Hill?"

Molly sighed. "My boss fired me when I didn't show up for work because Johnny and I eloped." Molly turned back to Janey, looking even more stressed-out. "Anyway, what kind of help are you looking for?"

"An experienced pastry chef," Janey said.

Molly's face fell.

"But I'll ask around, see if I know anyone who is hiring," Janey volunteered gently, sorry she couldn't help the young girl. "It's possible my mother might be able to use you over at The Wedding Inn, especially since you've worked there before in years past."

"Thanks. I know Johnny is looking for work, too," Molly said, cheeks pinkening self-consciously.

"Speaking of Johnny," Thad asked his younger sibling casually, "how was that honeymoon?"

To his and Janey's mutual horror, Molly burst into tears.

Chapter Ten

"It can't be that dire," Thad said, wrapping his arms around his sister.

"But it is!" Molly wailed, her hysteria building with every second that passed.

Janey brought a stool for Molly to sit on. "Maybe you should tell us about it," Janey coaxed softly, remembering how lost and alone she had felt after her own elopement years before.

Molly sobbed all the harder. "I wish I had n-n-never told Johnny that I was pregnant."

Well, this explained things, Janey thought. The hurry. The guilt. The confusion.

"Exactly how far along are you?" Thad asked, exchanging concerned glances with Janey over Molly's head.

"That's just it. I'm n-n-not going to have a baby!" Molly's shoulders heaved with the force of her crying. "I just thought I was."

"Slow down and start from the beginning," Janey urged quietly. She got a bottle of water out of the fridge and handed it to Molly, along with a box of Kleenex.

Molly wiped her eyes and spoke in a muffled voice. "It was a couple of weeks ago. My period didn't come and I got scared. So I got one of those drugstore tests and it said I was, and Johnny said we had to get married right away for the baby's sake. So we just went to Gatlinburg that night and saw a justice of the peace."

"When did you realize you weren't pregnant?" Janey asked.

"The day after we told all our parents about eloping. I woke up and I had started my period."

"So Johnny knows," Thad ascertained, still struggling to understand.

Panic lit her eyes. "No, I mean I couldn't tell him! Especially after—he's going to think I tricked him, and I didn't!"

"You have to tell him the truth, Molly."

"But he'll break up with me," Molly predicted miserably, as a new flood of tears rolled down her cheeks.

"You don't know that," Janey soothed, patting her shoulder.

"Yes, I do." Molly sniffed. "Johnny was losing interest in me before all this. And I could tell he didn't really want to marry me, even when we were saying our vows. And it's only gotten worse since we got back from Gatlinburg. He tries to hide it but whenever I look at him I just know he feels so trapped."

An emotion Janey was well acquainted with herself.

"Where is Johnny now?" Thad asked.

Molly blew her nose then let her hand fall to her lap desultorily. "Over at his parents' house," she said as she systematically shredded the used tissue in her lap.

"Do you want me to go with you?" Thad asked.

Molly shook her head. Sadness filled her eyes as she composed herself once again. "That would only make things worse. This is going to be awful enough." Molly paused. "I'll call him and ask him to come over here now."

AFTER THAD'S sister talked to her husband alone, Thad insisted upon driving her back to Chapel Hill. He didn't think she should be behind the wheel of a car in her upset state, and Janey agreed. So they took off, and Janey finished up at the bakery and headed home. She was just turning into her own driveway, a little more than an hour later, when Thad's SUV pulled up at the curb.

Wondering if something else had happened, she walked over to the passenger side. He let the window down. "Everything okay?" she asked.

"I thought it might take you a bit to wind down," he said, pointing to the bags of take-out on the seat beside him.

Janey could see he wanted to talk. "Come on in," she said. She wanted to talk to him, too. "So how was she?'' Janey asked, switching on the minimum of lights once they were inside the house.

Concern lit his handsome features. ''Better, when I dropped her off.'' However, he looked even more worried. ''I imagine she'll be a wreck tomorrow.''

''You think they'll end the marriage?'' Janey asked, her stomach growling she was so hungry.

Thad shook his head and opened up the bags. The aroma of spicy Mexican food surrounded them as she went to get two stoneware plates and some silverware for them. ''I don't know.''

Janey touched the side of his face and did her best to console him. ''I'm sorry that Molly's gone through such an ordeal, but maybe it's for the best.''

Thad handed her a Mexican beer, opened one for himself. ''How do you mean?''

Janey took a sip of the deliciously mellow brew. ''Well, they never should have gotten married just for the baby's sake.'' Janey had stayed with Ty for that reason and it had been a disaster in terms of their husband-wife relationship.

As Thad spread the food out on the coffee table, she got out a few pillows, and turned on some soft music to further set the relaxing mood. ''I've seen it work,'' Thad disagreed, ''as long as the parents get along and enjoy each other's company—and get along sexually, and all that.'' He looked at her levelly. ''Kids come first. At least that's the way it should be in this life. For instance,'' he said, sitting down on the floor in front of the sofa with a pillow behind his back, "it's obvious you put Chris way ahead of your own needs, and I admire that."

"You do, do you?" Janey teased as she kicked off her shoes. She had been wearing the same gray sheath dress all day, even back at the bakery. The only difference was now she didn't have a chef's coat on over top of it, to protect it from stains and spills.

"Yeah," Thad said as she sank down beside him. He reached over and put a pillow behind her, too, his capable hands brushing her spine as he made sure she was comfortable. "Too many kids are going without the love they should have these days. And it's a shame."

Janey couldn't disagree with Thad on that.

She looked over at the metal take-out pans with the snug-fitting cardboard tops that were spread out over the large rectangular coffee table. One touch and she knew it was all still piping hot. "So what have we got here?" It looked as if Thad had gotten enough to feed six, instead of just the two of them.

The way he looked at her then, as if he wanted to make love to her then and there, had Janey's pulse racing. "I didn't know what you liked so I ordered one of everything on the menu," he said.

She grinned, her mouth watering for a bite of the delicious food. And something much more intimate for dessert. "I see you've got your bases covered."

"I try," he admitted with a modest wink that sent her senses into overdrive.

"So how come you didn't tell me what you were up to today?" he asked as they divvied up a tamale and four kinds of enchiladas. "I could have gotten you an appointment to see Saul."

Janey had figured as much.

"But you didn't ask." Thad looked at her as if his feelings were hurt. "How come?"

It was Janey's turn to shrug. "I didn't want to appear to be taking advantage of our...um...dalliances."

"Dalliances?" he parroted humorously. "It's been a while since I've heard that word."

Janey ducked her head self-consciously. "Well, get used to it, because that's how I would describe it," she said as she concentrated on serving them both some rice.

He waited until she had finished, then tucked a finger beneath her chin and turned her face to his. "Nothing more than that?"

Janey swallowed around the parched feeling in her throat. "What else could it be?" she asked huskily.

He didn't flinch. "A prelude to something more... permanent."

Janey flushed, not sure if he was talking marriage or a long-term sexual affair. Both possibilities scared her, albeit for very different reasons. "We haven't known each other for very long." A matter of days. And yet, she thought silently to herself, it felt as though he had been a part of her life forever.

Thad regarded her confidently. "At our age we don't have to know each other for months and months to know what we think or feel. People with our experience have enough street smarts to size a person up pretty quickly.''

So they were both trustworthy individuals, responsible adults who tried their hardest not to trample on the feelings of others. So what? She slanted him a teasing glance in an effort to lighten the mood, and chided playfully in her best Miss Scarlett accent, ''Coach Lantz. Are you trying to make time with me again?''

He waggled his eyebrows at her. ''What do you think?'' He leaned seductively close.

Janey inhaled the familiar fragrance of his aftershave, and beneath that the intoxicatingly male scent of his skin. She batted her eyelashes at him, drawled sexily, ''I think you're trouble with a capital *T*.''

''Hmm. First time I've been called that.'' He looked as if he liked it, then leaned closer and studied her even more intently. ''Is that why you've been avoiding me?'' he asked, his shoulder rubbing hers. ''Because you think I am going to somehow lead you astray?''

The man definitely saw too much of what was in her heart and head. She gestured helplessly, aware it would do her absolutely no good to try and deny it, since that horse was long out of the barn. ''I think you've already done that, haven't you?'' she asked.

His eyes sparkled with unmistakably ardent lights. ''I think you've already done that, too, or was that *me* dropping my robe the other night?''

Unbidden, the image of the two of them making love flashed in her mind, bringing forth yet another thrill. One the more practical side of Janey knew would be wise not to repeat.

Janey held up both hands in mea culpa, determined to be as honest and forthright with him as she wanted him to be with her, now that the moment for truth-telling was upon them. "Okay, okay. I admit I am just as guilty for the impulsive behavior between us the last two weeks as you are. But that does not mean you have to keep calling or sticking around," she told him soberly, wanting to be clear about this much. "I'm a big girl. I may not play sports, but I do know the score."

"And what would that be?" he asked, no small trace of irony in his voice.

Heat climbed to her face. As much as she tried she could not bring herself to look him in the eye as she confessed in a low, strangled tone, "I've never had a lot of luck holding a guy's interest long-term. Sexually, anyway. So I would understand if you want to move on. There would be no hard feelings." Just a broken heart on my part, she added ruefully, doing her best to keep her face absolutely expressionless.

He ignored the release she had just given him as his eyes narrowed in obvious disbelief. "What about your husband?" Thad demanded curiously.

"Ty would rather have skied any day, anywhere, than make love with me. And after Chris was born, we hardly ever touched each other." She had never told that to another living soul. It had been just too humiliating. But somehow it was freeing, saying it to Thad.

He blinked at her. "You're serious."

"Painfully so. Which explains my morph into the hot chick who has no earthly idea what she is really doing. I guess I had something to prove to myself the other night." Like maybe it wasn't me, after all. It was Ty. She swallowed hard around the growing knot of emotion in her throat. "And so if you want to back out now. If you don't want to be with a—a—"

"Sex-starved lonely widow and mother of a twelve-year-old boy who spends all her time baking up a storm?"

The laughter in his voice brought a deeper blush to her cheeks. She reprimanded with mock sternness, "I was going to say novice."

Again, he took offense. He peered at her as if she had lost her mind. "Are you kidding?" He leaned even closer, as if that somehow would clear the mystery up.

"You may have noticed in our two dalliances, that you were the one with all the fancy moves. Not me."

"Hey, I'm an equal opportunity lover. Just so you know."

What the hell was that? Besides a rather obvious invitation to make a fool of herself over him yet again. "Thanks," Janey said dryly. "And now that we've cleared that up—" Hands flat on the coffee table, Janey started to rise.

Thad pulled her right back down beside him. "First of all, you're no novice," he soothed as he wrapped his hands around her shoulders. Moving closer, he spoke to her the way he spoke to one of his players

during a game. With utter concentration and serious-
ness. "The key to lovemaking is the same as any
other sport. The thing that matters, the thing that
makes everything work is right in here." He took her
right hand in his and laid it over her left breast. Looking deep into her eyes, he told her firmly, "You've
got the strongest heart of anyone I know. And heart
is what it takes."

JANEY HAD NO IDEA how he had managed it, but five
minutes later, the dinner mess was cleared away and
she was up in her bedroom with Thad.

"Haven't you heard?" she asked a little nervously,
now that the moment for further intimacy was upon
them. "I turn into an uptight mother of one at the
stroke of midnight, so—" Run, while you still can.

"So, relax." His sexy smile promised her everything she had ever longed for and more. His gaze
drifted over her lazily, head to toe, making leisurely
stops at breasts, waist, hips, thighs. "We're going to
have fun."

"Are we?" she asked, her voice soft, tentative. Or
were they heading for an on-ice collision of a broken
heart—hers—and crushed expectations—his? Doing
this on the spur of the moment, without thinking or
weighing consequences was one thing. Doing it
knowingly, deliberately, was quite another.

"Mmm-hmm." His expression hungry, he took her
hand in his and led her toward the neatly made covers
of her bed.

She watched, pulse racing, as he lifted his knit shirt

over his head and let it fall to the floor. Outwardly, she was still fighting it. Inwardly, she secretly liked the way he was taking charge. Tearing her glance away from his impossibly broad shoulders and nicely sculpted chest, she regarded him disdainfully. "I thought I indicated to you we wouldn't be doing this." That, under the complicated circumstances of their acquaintance, they would be better off as friends. Because if she were to let herself touch that warm, satiny smooth skin... Or be held against what even now she could see was going to be quite some arousal...her reckless streak would be back, full force. Never to be tamed again.

Thad traced the shape of her face with the palm of his hand, regarding her with unmistakable pleasure all the while. "I thought I indicated to you we would."

Tingles of warmth shimmied through her. "Do you always have to have your way?" she asked, unable to help but notice how handsome he looked in the soft glow of her bedside lamp. How determined. How very male.

"When it comes to you and this—always." He took the clip from her hair, watching as the heavy length of it fell to her shoulders in silky chestnut waves. "Got a problem with that?"

"Yes." She spread her hands over the satiny smooth skin and the light mat of crisp, curly hair, holding him at bay. "No. I don't know. Maybe."

He grinned, amused at the confusion in her tone. "Just so we know where we stand."

They were teetering on the edge of a cliff, safety

and practicality on one side, danger and unbelievable pleasure on the other. Should she throw caution to the wind and permanently become the wild woman Thad was urging her to be? Or stay as invulnerable—and lonely and unfulfilled—as she was? The only thing she knew for sure was that tonight was a turning point for them. Making love again would move them from fling to something more.

And Thad seemed to know it, too. Eyes darkening, he tugged her all the way against him and whispered, "I want to kiss you, Janey."

And she wanted to kiss him, common sense be damned.

His mouth came down on hers and he kissed her soundly, not stopping until her capitulation was complete and she felt the traitorous weakening of her knees. He drew back, his gaze ardently tracing her face, lingering on each feature in turn. "That was pretty good." His tongue traced her collarbone before moving to the sensitive spot behind her ear. "Now it's your turn," he said as an ache began to speed through her. "You kiss me."

Janey cupped his head in her hands, more than up to the challenge of his sexy coaching. "Okay." She went up on tiptoe, fitting her lips to his. She had expected him to be passive and he was for about a moment, and then his tongue twined with hers and his lips covered hers in a desperation and hunger that she not only understood but felt, too. Life wasn't simple. Neither was this. Lovemaking didn't come without consequences, but sometimes those consequences were worth the risk.

Hand to her spine, Thad lowered her to the bed.

He stretched out beside her, his lips moving down the nape of her neck, across her shoulders, to her breasts. He caressed her breasts through the fabric of her dress, with both palms, then laved the nipples with his tongue until they were tight and achy. He cupped the weight of them in his hands, brushed his thumbs across the tips. Kissed and suckled them again and again and again. Janey had never felt anything so wonderful and she moaned as fire swept through her middle, pooling low.

She wanted him to take her—now. But she also wanted to be an equally adept lover. And that meant giving, as well as receiving. She shifted positions, turning so that he was beneath her. "My turn."

He lay back against the pillows, arms folded beneath his head. Waiting. Janey stretched out on top of him. Her heart fluttered once in anticipation, then she kissed him, long and slow and sweet. Hard and deep. Wet and hot. She kissed him until her heartbeat hammered in her ears and she was so aroused she could barely think. And then she did what he had done. She slid lower, letting her lips explore the strong column of his throat, his collarbone, the mat of hair across his chest. She found his flat male nipples, hidden in the crisp hair, and she kissed and touched those, too, until they were as hard and tight as her own, until he groaned his pleasure just as she had, and then she moved lower still. Letting her hair slide across his abdomen like a sensual ribbon, teasing, caressing, as her hands found the fly on his jeans. He tried to stop her, tried to take control once again, but she wouldn't let him, and as she stripped him of the rest of his clothes, he finally let her do what she pleased.

Still in her dress and panty hose, she knelt between his legs, running her hands over the bunched muscles of his thighs, the flatness of his abdomen. She found the cleft between his buttocks, the sensitive area beneath his sex. She traced the length of his erection, the nest of curls at the base, the drop of fluid at the tip. And then she did it all again, cupping the fertile sacs with one hand, caressing him with the other, using her lips and tongue over the shaft. She wanted to drive him to completion, and she knew he was nearly there. Then his hands were on her shoulders, Janey was on her back and he was the one shifting over top of her.

"Oh, no you don't," he said.

"But—"

"Not without you."

Janey meant to argue, but the need on his face, the passion in his kiss, soon had her surrendering to his will. She gave in to the plundering rhythm he set, allowing him to slide his hands beneath her and unzip her dress, ease it off. Panty hose, bra, panties followed. Soon she was as naked as he. And as aroused. She didn't need the intimate caress of his fingers or the sweep of his tongue, but he gave it to her anyway, not stopping until she was shuddering and falling apart. And only then, when she was aching for him, rising up, half mad with desire, did he slide her up into a half-sitting position on the pillows, and struggle to find a condom.

Heat flowing through her, she helped him sheath himself. His gaze locked with hers, he slid between her thighs and pulled her legs to his waist. Her leg muscles tensed as he used his fingers to ease the way, and then they were one again, the delicious waves of pleasure building, plunging her over the edge. She urged him on with her body and her moans, meeting him stroke for stroke. Their bodies collided again and again. He was hard and heavy and hot atop her as he laid claim to her with predatory possessiveness. Her back arched. Her thighs fell even farther apart. Blood rushed hot and needy through her veins. And then all was dissolving as they moved together toward a single goal, finding it, clinging to it, savoring the release. They clung together that way, trembling, bodies hot and throbbing. And then he kissed her again. Softer now. And in that instant, with satisfaction rushing through her, Janey knew. There could be no more denying it. Complications be damned. She could really, really get used to this.

FOR THAD THE AFTERMATH of sex had always meant deep, immediate sleep. Until now. With Janey cuddled in his arms, her body still trembling hotly, the sweetness of their lovemaking still fresh on his mind, the last thing he wanted to do was slip into oblivion.

Especially when he knew their chances to be together like this would not extend beyond the week.

Unless he could convince her to really throw caution to the wind and jump ahead to where they were going to end up anyway.... As Janey snuggled closer, Thad wondered if her thoughts were going in the same inevitable direction as his. Still stroking her hair, he decided to find out. "Contemplating how long you need before we go again?" he teased. He knew he was. He had never felt as happy as he did when he was with her.

Janey lifted her head, affection shining in her amber eyes. "Give me a break, Coach. I haven't had a cardio workout like that since...well, I don't know when."

To his disappointment, his gut told him this wasn't the time. But soon, he promised himself. Very soon. "Not much for exercising?" he chided lightly, tightening his arms around her.

"I used to be." Janey sighed contentedly as she rubbed a caressing hand across his chest. "But then when we moved here, there didn't seem to be any time to go running anymore."

Thad knew the lack of regular exercise could be adding to her stress. "Why not early in the mornings before work?" he suggested gently, realizing that was something else they could do together, and a surefire way to bring her around to his way of thinking.

Janey shrugged. "I'm busy getting Chris off to school or whatever."

She shouldn't be making excuses when it came to

her health. "Not tomorrow," Thad pointed out. "He's at camp."

She made a face as he deftly robbed her of the ability to procrastinate. "But I've got to be in the bakery by eight."

Thad grinned. "So I'll go with you at six," he offered cheerfully, thinking how pretty she looked with her hair all tousled, the color of exertion in her cheeks. "I'll even buy you breakfast."

She tilted her head and regarded him thoughtfully. "I'm not sure I can keep up with you."

She'd managed so far just fine, Thad thought. He bent and kissed her tenderly. "Why don't you just let me worry about that?"

THE NEXT MORNING, running along the jogging paths that wound throughout the narrow park that went from one end of town to the other and ran alongside several miles of Holly Creek, Janey was surprised to see so many people out. But Thad, who ran the trails all the time, obviously knew that was the case.

As they jogged down the paved path, at a much slower pace than Thad was used to keeping, she looked over at him and remarked, "You wanted to be seen with me, didn't you?"

He grinned and didn't deny it.

"What is this—a territorial thing?" Janey huffed and puffed as she stopped by a grouping of picnic tables and pulled out the plastic water bottle she had strapped to her waist. She was really beginning to feel this run in her legs. Or maybe it was the lovemaking from the night before she was beginning to feel. Before the night was over, they had tried several new—for her anyway—and interesting positions. Which had left her body aching pleasurably in a few other places, as well.

Thad watched as she took a long thirsty drink. "Maybe. Do you mind?"

Actually, she didn't. And that surprised Janey, too. Because broadcasting her ongoing relationship with Thad was bound to invite even more commentary from her family. Nevertheless, she rather liked feeling as if she belonged to him. Because that was certainly how Thad was acting.

Several voices had them turning. Janey blinked. "Hey, isn't that your dad over there?" she asked, recognizing the man in the sport shirt and khakis, a cup of coffee in his hand.

Thad looked at the handsome couple, standing side by side. "He probably came out here to watch the sunrise."

"And your mom?" Janey asked, noting Veronica was clad in shorts and a T-shirt similar to Janey's own. His mother was in her mid-to-late fifties, but she had the body of a much younger woman.

"She's really into running, always has been," Thad explained as they stood for a moment, catching their breath, while Veronica and Gordon continued to talk.

"You see it, too, don't you?" Thad remarked quietly after a moment.

Janey nodded. "The way your dad looks at your mom…" Most divorced couples she knew were acrimonious even years after the fact. Not Veronica Lauder and Gordon Lantz. He still looked completely besotted with his ex. While Veronica simply looked...friendly, in a casual, noncommittal sort of way.

Thad sighed, and borrowed Janey's bottle. "He's still in love with her. Always has been, and according to him anyway, always will be."

Janey watched Thad take a long drink. She knew that had to be so hard for him, because he obviously loved both his parents, as well as his stepfather, Lionel Lauder. "Why did your parents divorce, if you don't mind my asking?"

Thad wiped his lips with the back of his hand. "They married too young, chiefly because I was on the way. They thought they could make it work, but after I was born my mother realized she was never going to love my father the way he should be loved, so she asked him for a divorce."

"And he agreed," Janey guessed.

"Not right away." Thad frowned, handing her water back to her. "I think it took a couple of years for my mom to convince my father he wasn't going to be able to turn things around for them romantically. The problem never was a lack of attention or chivalry on his part, just a lack of feeling on hers."

Which was, Janey thought, the kind of thing you can't fix. Her heart went out to Thad—obviously his parents' divorce still hurt on some level.

"Anyway," Thad continued, in a low, brooding tone, "she eventually found the kind of passionate love she was looking for with my stepfather, Lionel. But my dad is still carrying the torch.''

''And you wish he'd stop.''

Thad wiped the sweat from his brow with the hem of his T-shirt. ''I just think it's a hell of a waste,'' he said in obvious frustration, ''to go through life yearning after someone who doesn't yearn after you. They would both be better off if my dad just cut his losses and walked away.''

''Which is what you did in your own divorce,'' Janey said softly, admiring Thad's guts—in ending his marriage and putting closure to it as Renee asked—even as she felt for the hurt Thad had endured in the process. Maybe if she had done the same regarding her union with Ty, they would have been happier. Chris, too. Because staying locked in a loveless marriage was no example to set for her son. She knew that now. And though it was too late to change what had happened in the past, she knew she could control what she did in the future.

Thad nodded, his expression grim but determined. ''I promised myself a long time ago I would never make my dad's mistake, by hanging on to something that was never meant to be in the first place.'' He looked at Janey seriously. ''It's a vow I mean to keep.''

Chapter Eleven

"Chris is making amazing progress, isn't he?" Dylan Hart said as he and Janey sat in the practice facility and watched the hockey game in progress.

Janey turned to her sportscaster brother. Dylan had been in Carolina taping an interview with a university coach who summered there. He'd dropped by to cheer on his nephew on his next to last day of summer camp, before heading back to Chicago.

"Is that a professional opinion or family pride speaking?" Janey teased.

Dylan squinted at her. As always, he was awesomely attired, in a suit and tie custom-tailored for his six-foot frame. The smallest of all five Hart brothers, he was also the most sophisticated and had made the transition from small-town boy to big-city sportscaster with ease.

"Even you have to admit this week at hockey camp has been good for Chris," Dylan chided, casting another admiring glance his nephew's way. "He's made great strides in his skating. And the way he handles a puck now shows real discipline. That plus his talent—he could go places one day if he keeps up this level of intensity."

Janey kept her eyes on the action on the ice. Thad was out there, along with his assistant coaches, giving the kids pointers as the play progressed. They were all looking up at him like he was the greatest man on earth. She understood the feeling well.

"And I'm not just talking about his hockey playing, Janey," Dylan continued. "I had dinner with Chris and some of his buddies before the game. He told me he was doing better in his math class, too."

Janey knew she owed Thad for that. "Thad worked with him on that, the week before camp," she said.

Dylan lifted a curious brow.

Janey continued. "In addition to helping with the lessons, Thad made Chris understand that he's going to need math if he wants to keep his options open."

Dylan looked as pleased as Janey. "That has to make you happy."

Janey turned her glance back to Thad, noting how handsome he looked in his coaching attire. "Chris has needed someone who could get through to him, since Ty died. Thad's managed to do that."

"Which isn't a surprise," Dylan mentioned, with his usual enthusiasm for all things that had to do with sports. "Thad has a reputation for working wonders with players. He has a way of sizing people up, giving them exactly what they need to motivate them to perform."

Janey thought about the lovemaking session she

and Thad'd had the night before. It had been amazing. She'd felt wilder, more uninhibited than she ever had in her life. Under his tutelage, it had been so easy to let go of her shyness and self-consciousness and really come into her own in bed. And he'd done the same thing for her in her professional life, by prodding her to drop the woe-is-me act and find a way to expand her business so it would give her the financial return she needed.

"And it's not just in a hockey arena." Dylan shook his head with obvious respect. "A couple of years ago, Thad headed up a charity drive for the children's hospital in Nashville—that's where he was coaching then—and he got people who never got involved in that kind of thing to not only sign up for it, but work their tail ends off. They raised a record amount of money for the hospital. People are still talking about it. They don't know how he did it."

Janey did. Thad had a way of bringing out the best in people.

"All that's ever necessary is for Thad to figure out what he wants. And then he knows exactly what to do to get it."

Dylan turned to Janey. "You're lucky he's taken such an interest in Chris. Something like this could make all the difference in his life."

And mine, Janey thought.

"YOU'RE AWARE this is our last night like this," Thad whispered in Janey's ear that evening as they cuddled together in his bed.

Her body still humming from the sensual after-shocks of their lovemaking, Janey burrowed deeper into the warm protective curve of his arm. She wanted to stay here with him like this forever, but she knew she couldn't. This week had been like a wonderful romantic dream for her, but soon it was back to life as usual with her parental responsibilities taking up the forefront of her life. Between that and the de-mands of running her business, she would barely have time for herself, never mind her newfound love affair with Thad. She propped herself up on her elbow and looked over at Thad wistfully, wondering if he was as sad as she was that this passionate respite was all about to come to an end. "Chris comes home from camp late tomorrow. Which means—"

Thad nodded, understanding. "You won't be spending the night with me or vice versa."

"Right." Janey swallowed around the sudden ache in her throat, the feeling of loss deep inside her. "I wouldn't want Chris to think it's okay to have ca-sual—"

Thad pressed a silencing finger to her lips. His blue eyes were dark, serious as he corrected, "There's nothing casual about what I feel for you, Janey."

Nor I you, Janey thought, very much aware that even though they had made love at least a dozen times in days and nights gone by, they had yet to say the words that would have lifted their liaison from some-thing purely sexual and sensual to something more. To something even the most old-fashioned side of her would have approved. "You know what I mean," Janey said, ducking her head.

Silence fell between them as Janey lay back against the pillows and drew her forearm across her eyes.

Thad turned onto his side and gently brought her forearm down to her side. "I know we haven't been seeing each other all that long."

He'd come into her life two weeks ago and nothing had been the same since.

"But I've never felt for any woman what I feel for you." He paused, looked deep into her eyes. "And I think your feelings for me are just as intense."

Janey's heart began to pound as she thought about the words she still yearned to hear from the man she felt like she had been waiting for her entire life. "What are you trying to say?" she asked him hoarsely, wondering if this was it, the moment when all her dreams really were going to come true.

The smile on Thad's lips reached his eyes as he laid out his thoughts as pragmatically as any business deal. "I think we should get married."

JANEY HAD EXPECTED a lot of things from Thad Lantz. A proposal wasn't one of them. And yet she knew, he wasn't doing this impulsively. Unlike her, he was not prone to cycles of recklessness and regret.

"We're too old to sneak around," Thad continued persuading her calmly. He lifted the back of her hand to his lips and kissed it warmly. "And frankly there's no reason for us to limit ourselves to a love affair. What I feel for you and Chris isn't going to change,

Janey. I know what I want—the three of us to be a family and have a happy, stable life.''

Janey knew she loved Thad. She had been waiting her entire life to love and be loved by someone like him. But she wasn't so sure if he actually loved her. Oh, she knew he cared about her and her son, and that he desired her. She knew he was a good, kindhearted, stand-up kind of guy who would never cheat on her or be anything but totally responsible and wonderful to her and Chris. She knew, if she married him, he would see she and Chris had everything they wanted and needed. But was it enough without the words? Without him actually being in love with her and not averse to telling her so?

On the other hand, she told herself practically, words were cheap. Ty had said he loved her many times in the beginning, but Ty's actions had never owned up to that grand pronouncement, and she had been miserable as a result.

Janey's heart told her that Thad would never treat her or Chris badly. He had too much character to be anything but trustworthy. And what was it Thad had said to her about listening to her gut, about not thinking something to death but just following her heart and doing what felt right? This felt right.

He kissed her brow, her cheek, the nape of her neck, the sensitive spot behind her ear. And then finally, finally, her lips. ''I don't want things to go back the way they were, with me inventing reasons to see you or drop by, and not being able to kiss you and hold you and make love to you every night,'' he told her as he kissed her collarbone, the curve of her shoulder, the underside of her wrist. "Practice starts in August. The first preseason game's in September. And I'm going to be on the road a lot with the team the months after that."

Janey knew it was a long season. The Storm played some eighty games at home and away, and that was before the playoff rounds started, which would not conclude until June.

Thad took her in his arms again, and fit his arousal against her softness. "If we're married, you and Chris can come with me some of the time. I promise you, I'll never let either of you down, the way Ty did."

What was she waiting for? Janey wondered, already tingling all over in anticipation of their making love again. So what if he hadn't said he loved her yet? He had showed her how much he cared for her and her son in every way that counted. And you did only live once. This was it. Her chance for happiness, and her son's. "Yes," Janey said, her eyes brimming with heartfelt joy as she wrapped both her arms around his neck and kissed him soundly, sealing the deal. "I will marry you, as soon as you want." As soon as we can.

Thad smiled, abruptly looking as happy and excited about their future as she felt. "Then we'll tell Chris tomorrow?" he asked, as he rolled her over onto her back, and kissed his way down her throat.

Janey nodded blissfully. "Right after I pick him up from camp..."

JANEY KNEW something was wrong when her brother Fletcher walked into the bakery Friday morning. The most easygoing of all the Hart men, Fletcher usually had a smile on his face and a welcoming light in his eyes. Now, he just looked grim.

"Shouldn't you be over at the vet clinic?" she asked, glancing at her watch. It was barely eleven and he should still be seeing his veterinary patients. Instead, he was standing there in front of her in jeans, chambray shirt and boots.

"Cal called me and asked me to come and get you."

Janey tensed at the worry in his golden brown eyes. "Something happen to Mom?"

"Mom's fine." Fletcher ran a hand through his shaggy honey-brown hair and looked even more reluctant as he told her, "It's Chris. He had a little mishap this morning during his game."

Mishap. Janey's heart skidded to a halt. Suddenly, she couldn't move, couldn't think, could barely breathe. "How bad is it?" she asked anxiously, suddenly furious that she had allowed her brothers to talk her into letting him attend camp.

Fletcher closed the distance between them and wrapped a strong arm around her. He smelled like antiseptic and some sort of topical medicine and he had a streak of what looked to be mud across one sleeve.

"Chris tried to avoid slamming into someone and ran into another player instead and then hit the boards."

Janey recalled how fast and she now saw—recklessly—her son had been skating the night before and could only imagine the force with which her son had crashed into the wall. She could only hope he hadn't suffered a terrible head or neck injury or been cut by the blades on someone else's skates in the process. "Does he have a concussion?" she demanded.

Fletcher frowned. "They don't know. He passed out briefly, but that might have been from pain. Joe rode with him in the ambulance and Cal's evaluating him now over at the medical center."

Oh, God. Please. Let him be okay. Tears blurred her eyes. "I've got to go to him," Janey struggled with the pastel pink apron over her white chef's coat.

"Maybe we should turn off these ovens first," Fletcher moved past her.

Stricken, Janey turned her glance in her brother's direction.

"Got a couple cakes in here, I see." Fletcher opened the door and peered into the oven.

Seven, to be exact, Janey thought, as she struggled to get a grip on her emotions. Chances were Chris was going to be just fine, she told herself sternly. "It's a wedding cake," she said evenly. "It has to be ready tomorrow and it's only half-baked." If she took the layers out now, it would be ruined. She would have to start all over. And yet, to wait...

"How much longer?" Fletcher asked crisply.

Barely able to remember her own name at that point, Janey glanced at the timer. "Twenty minutes."

"I'll call one of my vet techs, and have them come

over and take them out. They can stay here with the shop until you get back.''

''Thanks,'' Janey said gratefully. There were times when it was nice to have brothers who didn't mind stepping in to take command of a situation. This was one of them.

Fletcher made the call as they walked out to his extended cab pickup truck. It was covered with what looked to be wet mud. ''House call,'' he said in explanation of the mess.

Janey nodded, knowing Fletcher spent as much time out at the farms and ranches in the area as he did in the office. ''Who contacted you about Chris?''

''Thad.'' Fletcher backed out of the space while they were still fastening their safety belts. ''He didn't want you getting the news over the phone. He knew you'd be upset and he was afraid you'd jump in the car and have a wreck on the way over to the medical center.''

She probably would have.

''Is Joe still with Chris?'' Janey asked, knowing local EMT policy was that only family members could ride in the ambulance with the patient. So Thad wouldn't have been able to accompany Chris to the Emergency Room in any case.

Not that this would have been a big deal to someone like Thad, who saw injured players all the time and was used to sending them off to the hospital in an ambulance and getting a report back later once the player was evaluated by medical professionals.

''No. Joe went back to the camp as soon as he

handed him over to Cal. It's the last day. And they've got a big luncheon and award ceremonies going on.''

"So Joe was needed there, as was Thad."

And what about Chris, Janey wondered. What did Chris need? And why hadn't she taken the day off work and been there, watching the last of the camp's exhibition games? Had she not been making love with Thad last night, she could have done her baking during the previous evening, and been there for her son when he needed her....

"Thad said to tell you he would catch up with the two of you as soon as he could. And to call him if there are any problems. Not that he expected any since Cal is in charge of Chris's medical care." Fletcher reached across the seat and awkwardly patted her hand, then put his pickup into Drive. "Chris is going to be okay, Janey."

"I know," she replied firmly even though she knew no such thing. She had to keep a positive attitude. Had to, had to, had to....

Chris looked as if he were surviving the ordeal when she entered the examination room in the Emergency Room at Holly Springs Regional Medical Center. If you considered the fact his skin was ashen gray, he had a cut, swollen lip, and was still in such pain he seemed incapable of speech. Janey could tell her son had been crying. He never cried. And wouldn't appreciate her doing so, either.

Struggling to contain her own worries, she walked over to him. He looked gangly and vulnerable in the hospital gown. The sheet was drawn up to his waist, and one side was bunched up over what looked to be some rather significant ice packs. "Hey." She issued the standard North Carolina greeting.

Chris ducked his head and said nothing as he studiously rubbed the sheet between his thumb and forefinger. A single tear slid out of the corner of one eye. Janey's throat ached as she struggled to hold back her own tears.

"What's going on?" Janey continued in the most normal tone she could manage.

Chris shrugged and turned his glance to the wall. The look on his face was stubborn and unhappy. It reminded Janey a lot of Ty whenever Ty had suffered a setback in his never-realized quest to make it to the Olympics. A shiver of dread curled in her stomach. It was this very road she had wanted to avoid, when she had refused to let him attend camp and further his obsession in the first place.

Cal appeared in the doorway. He was dressed in surgical blue pants, shirt, and cap. With his gray eyes and traditionally-cut ash-blond hair, he looked the most like their late father of all the siblings. "Hey, sis. Talk to you for a minute?" he said amiably, the bedside manner he used on his patients and their families in good stead. Cal looked to their brother for help. "Fletcher—?"

"I'll stay with Chris," Fletcher volunteered.

Janey followed her brother down the hall to a room with lighted screens. He slapped a couple of pictures from the MRI that had been taken up on the screens and hit the lights. "Chris has what's commonly known as a groin injury."

"One of the most common in hockey," Janey said.

"And most painful," Cal agreed grimly. "It usually happens from a sudden start or stop or change in direction. And in Chris's case it was the latter two things. The muscle fibers are actually torn and not just stretched."

"Which means?" Janey asked, not sure what he was telling her.

"It's going to be a lot slower to heal."

A fact Chris was not going to appreciate. "How long are we talking?"

"Four, six weeks, maybe longer."

She thought about the bloody cut on her son's face. "*Did* he hit his head on the boards?" And if so, how could she have been foolish enough to allow this to happen? Hadn't she promised herself she would never let her son indulge in the kind of reckless athletic behavior his father had?

"Actually, we think he may have banged it a little on either the ice or the boards on the way down but in either case his helmet seems to have protected him just fine. Although he lost his mouth guard in the process, which is the reason for the cut lip."

Great, Janey thought. She supposed she should feel lucky her son still had all his teeth.

"Since it was an amateur game we don't have any instant replays to look at. And it all happens pretty quick. So it's just recollection of those close enough to be able to see."

Janey had seen her share of on-ice collisions in their brother Joe's games. It was frightening, even when you didn't have a personal connection with the players involved. "Fletcher said something about two other players," Janey said nervously. Were they here, too? And if so, what kind of shape were they in?

"They were both uninjured and were able to finish the game."

Which probably only added to her son's mortification, since he had been the only one to be carted off in an ambulance. Janey said a little prayer of thanks for the other boys' continued good health, then turned her attention back to her son's condition. "Fletcher also said Chris passed out."

"Very briefly. Probably from the pain of the muscle tear."

Janey could only imagine how excruciating that must have been. "But he's going to be okay."

"Yeah. I've got to warn you, though, his recovery isn't going to be fun. He's got torn muscle fibers that have to heal and then he's going to have to go into physical therapy to get his injured muscles back in playing shape. And for the first week or so any movement—walking, sitting, shifting positions in bed—is going to be very painful."

Janey tried to be grateful it wasn't any worse. "When can I take him home?"

Cal hesitated once again, looking even more reluctant as he wrapped an arm around her shoulders. "That, Janey, is what I have to talk to you about."

To HIS CHAGRIN, it was 7:00 p.m. before Thad was able to get away from the camp. Figuring Chris had long since been released from the Holly Springs Medical Center, Thad headed for Janey's. To his surprise, she didn't appear to be home. And she wasn't answering her cell phone, either. So he headed back along Main Street, and found her where he least expected her to be, at her bakery.

Janey barely looked up from the cake she was frosting when he walked in. She looked pale and exhausted, and he could hardly blame her for that. He knew she'd had quite a scare that morning—they all had. But her son was a tough kid and he would bounce back from this, the way all true athletes did.

"You're working tonight?" he asked in surprise.

She gave him a deeply disappointed look. "I have to finish this and take it to The Wedding Inn."

So she blamed him for Chris's injury. No surprise there. "Where's Chris?" Thad asked, determined to deal with this situation calmly, even if she wouldn't.

"With Cal, at his place," she retorted crisply. "He's off this weekend and he offered to take care of Chris."

Thad edged nearer. "I'm surprised you agreed to that," he said gently.

Hurt flashed in her amber eyes. "I didn't have much choice. Chris didn't want to come home with me."

It didn't take a rocket scientist to figure out why. "That's understandable." Thad did his best to help her see reason. "A groin injury is embarrassing under the best of circumstances. To be a twelve-year-old boy, with no dad in residence... He's obviously going to need some help getting around and getting the ice in the right place for a couple of days. It makes sense he wouldn't want his mother helping him with that if there were any other recourse.''

''That's what Cal said.'' She didn't look as if she had appreciated it any more coming from him than she did from Thad.

''You understand Cal is just trying to limit the humiliation of the ordeal for Chris,'' Thad explained as he attempted to comfort her by putting an arm around her shoulders.

Janey extricated herself from his arm and turned her back to him.

''Look, I know it's upsetting when an athlete gets hurt, and it's a million times worse when said athlete happens to be your son,'' Thad said as he watched her pipe icing onto the edges of the cake. ''And I'm sorry you had to go through it alone today.''

Janey lifted a hand to cut him off. ''I understand why you couldn't go to the medical center with Chris,'' she said bluntly.

She knew, as well as Thad, that the EMTs wouldn't have let him ride in the ambulance, and Cal had been right there for Chris when he arrived. Thad had made sure of that.

''I still want to tell him we're going to get married.'' Thad wanted to tell everyone. Make it official. Before she backed out. Because the way she was acting right now, he was pretty sure she wanted to back out.

Janey hesitated, for the first time since he had come in seeming a tad vulnerable, then her expression sobered. "Tonight probably isn't the time," she retorted matter-of-factly.

"It might give him something to look forward to," Thad suggested softly, ready to do anything that would help Janey and Chris feel better.

Janey shook her head. "It won't hurt us to wait. You'll see."

BUT IT DID HURT THEM, and by Wednesday evening, Thad knew he had to do something to keep from losing the woman in his life altogether. "You can't keep avoiding me," Thad told Janey when he caught up with her at 5:00 p.m.

"Look, my life is not so great right now," Janey said as she joined him on the sidewalk outside Delectable Cakes. Her face was pale. There were circles beneath her eyes, as if she hadn't been sleeping much, either. And he knew that expression on her face by now. There would be no backing down.

"Because of Chris's injury," he said.

"Because of a lot of things." She stepped past him, looking as self-sufficient and independent as ever. "I've got to get home."

Thad moved to block her way. "Uh, no, actually, you don't."

She lifted a brow at his temerity and explained with

barely veiled patience, "Chris is going to need dinner."

He stuck his thumbs in the loops on either side of his fly and rocked back on his heels. "Joe and Emma are going to handle that."

She blinked. Her expression held more challenge than warmth. "You called my brother and his wife," she repeated, dumbfounded.

Thad shrugged, not about to apologize for doing what had to be done. "I told them I needed to talk to you alone. They graciously agreed to feed and entertain Chris tonight, and regale him with tales of some of Joe's injuries and recuperation strategies while you and I have a nice quiet dinner at my place."

She stepped back a pace, color first fading, then coming into her face. "That's really not a good idea."

"Then we'll go to a restaurant," he said affably. "Your choice." The important thing was for them to start talking. Spending time with each other again.

Janey pressed her lips together. Her pretty chin took on that stubborn tilt he knew so well. "Not a good idea, either," she said.

"Then where?" Thad demanded in a flat, non-negotiable tone. He looked deep into her eyes. "Because we are going to talk, Janey." Whether you like it or not!

"Fine. I'll follow you to your house." She gave in with a beleaguered sigh and another stormy look. "But I'm only staying five minutes," she said.

Thad thought about the ring in his pocket and knew five minutes was all it would take.

JANEY HAD NEVER BEEN any good at rectifying the mistakes she made in her life. And she sensed tonight was going to be the hardest yet. Her suspicion was confirmed the moment she walked in and saw the dining-room table set for a romantic dinner for two.

She turned to Thad, not sure whose heart she was going to be breaking—his or hers. Just knowing, for all their sakes, it had to be done. And done soon.

She tried to break it to him as gently as she could. "I never should have started seeing you."

He eyed her cautiously. "Seeing me or sleeping with me?"

Leave it to him to try to boil it down to a mathematical problem he could solve. "Both," Janey said succinctly.

She drew a deep breath, and plunged on, more than ready to get this over with. "I thought I could handle it, if I set out certain boundaries, made certain allowances." Like the one that said it would be okay if she didn't require him to love her, that said it was okay for them to run their relationship and upcoming marriage like some sort of sophisticated arrangement. But Chris's injury had made her see that they were all still vulnerable anyway and feelings *were* involved. And it was that potential for hurt and spirit-crushing disillusionment that she couldn't allow. Not in her life. Or in Chris's. Not again. Now when they had already suffered so much.

Not that she expected Thad to understand.

He just saw what he wanted, and figured out how to get it.

But she couldn't do that. And neither could Chris.

She ducked her head and continued what she knew she had to say, "The same way I thought Chris could handle chasing his dream of becoming a pro hockey player one day."

Thad held out his hands beseechingly. "He can still do that."

"Physically, maybe," Janey allowed. She swallowed hard around the rising knot of emotion in her throat. "Emotionally, he's not any better equipped to handle setbacks than his father was."

Thad went very still, understanding at least some of what she was saying at long last. Concern etched on the handsome features of his face, he wrapped an arm around her shoulder and asked gently, "He's still not talking to you?"

Janey shrugged and struggled not to cry. "I guess that depends on whether you count monosyllables or not. He's stopped working hard at his math, too."

Thad paused, thinking. "Maybe he just needs some extra help."

"And maybe," Janey said, shooting Thad a resentful glance as she moved away from Thad's compelling touch, "Chris never should have started down this road in the first place."

Thad clamped his lips together. "And for that you blame me."

Janey lifted a hand, let it fall. She had to give credit

where it was due. "If you hadn't showed Chris's letter to Joe or pushed to have him go to camp—" she
accused hoarsely.

Thad frowned. "I would have broken his heart."

Janey sighed and rubbed a hand across the tense
muscles in the back of her neck. "It's broken now."

Thad's legendary patience began to fade as he
snapped, "He's twelve, Janey. All he knows is that
he didn't get to finish camp and he's got weeks of
physical therapy to complete. Once that is done, he'll
be good as new." Thad paused, looking her up and
down in a way that could not be described as anything
but critical. "But you won't be, will you?" He ad-
vanced on her, muscles tense. "All this time you've
been saying Chris can't take rejection when you're
the one with the problem. You're the one who falls
apart the first time you hit a bump in the road or meet
a little resistance."

Janey gasped in dismay. "That's not true."

He grasped her by the shoulders. "Then why are
you pushing me away?"

"Because I can't do this." Janey wrested free of
his grip and moved away. She threw up her hands in
frustration, angry that he wasn't letting this be a simple painless goodbye, angry that it hurt so damn
much. Angry most of all that she had let herself love
him more than life itself!

"Can't do what?" he stormed right back.

Sadness and regret colored her tone. "I can't pretend that you and I can just decide we want to be a
family and have it all magically work out. I can't

pretend that I can juggle all these balls, be a businesswoman and a baker and a mother and a lover to you, never mind a good wife, and succeed at any of it!''

Grimly, he looked her up and down. ''So you're afraid to risk your heart and open yourself up to marriage and family. At least over the long haul.''

Once again, Janey noted, Thad had said nothing about love. ''I am wary,'' Janey countered evenly, ''of making a mistake that is going to cost us all. Just because it was something I wanted to do at the moment. Like make love with you.''

''So in other words,'' Thad said slowly, looking more and more resentful with every second that passed, ''now that it's all becoming real—with problems and obstacles to overcome, instead of all heartwarming fantasy—you don't want any part of it.''

The ice in his voice chilled her to her very soul. Janey folded her arms in front of her. ''I wouldn't have put it that way. But yes,'' she said defensively, forcing herself to look him in the eye. ''You're right. Chris's mishap on the ice and his reaction to it have brought me back to reality.

''The hard fact is,'' she continued with heartfelt weariness, ''you've been as recklessly caught up in the one-solution-fits-all as I have been, thinking that in hooking up with each other and getting married, we would both magically have the ideal family we have both always wanted. You'd have a son again. Chris would have a father again, and I'd have someone to share parental responsibilities with. Heck, we'd even have a—a—'sex buddy' in the bargain.''

"A sex buddy!" Thad echoed furiously, as if he had never heard the term.

Janey flushed. "Well, what else would you call it?" she demanded, embarrassed beyond belief. "We've certainly never talked about love." Because if he had, things might have been different. But they weren't. And like it or not, Janey had to remind herself of that. Again and again and again, if necessary.

"So you're saying what? You want me out of your life?" he demanded irately.

"Yes," Janey snapped right back. The sooner the better. Before she broke down in front of him and started crying like there was no tomorrow. Because even if he didn't love her and never would, she did love him.

Thad continued facing her. He looked as he did at the end of a hockey game, when the chips were down, the seconds were ticking away. And he still hadn't given up, he was still sure with the right maneuvering he would bring his team to victory.

"I'm not abandoning Chris," he told her quietly after a moment. "I'm still going to be there for him if and when he needs a friend. Regardless of how you feel about me."

Janey knew he was trying to reassure her but it was the absolute worst thing to say. Because Janey had feared he only wanted a ready-made family all along. And now he was proving it to her, with his actions and attitude.

"As for us—" Thad's voice softened tenderly "—I think you should take your time and really think about this before you make a decision. You have what it takes to have a successful marriage with me, Janey. We both do."

He was talking to her as if this were a game or a mutually beneficial business deal.

"Right now, you're holding back, the way players do when they're in a slump and things aren't going their way."

Janey put up a hand, unable, unwilling to hear any more. "I know as a coach, you can usually do whatever is necessary to get what you need or want from people, Thad." *And that you usually succeed.* "Not from me. Not this time," she told him bitterly. Not ever.

Chapter Twelve

"It's over," Molly told Thad several days later, when she stopped by his office at the practice arena to see him. "Johnny and I called it quits, and we went to see a lawyer about a marriage dissolution."

Thad shut down his computer and pushed away from his desk. He wrapped his younger sister in a hug. "I'm sorry."

"It's okay." Molly leaned against him wearily. She stepped back and drew in an enervating breath. "I'm mostly relieved, anyway." Sadness filled her eyes. "We weren't ready to get married. We realized we don't even love each other anymore, at least not the way we should. Still," she bit her lip uncertainly, "it's going to be hard to tell Mom and Dad."

An understatement. During the years Molly and Johnny had been dating, Lionel and Veronica had become very fond of him and his family. "You want me to come with you?" Thad asked.

Molly nodded gratefully. "I could use a big brother about now."

Veronica and Lionel weren't as surprised by the news as Molly thought they would be.

"We knew something was wrong," Lionel said, when Molly had finished explaining everything to them. "We just couldn't figure out what."

Molly paused. "Then you're not mad at me?" she asked tentatively.

Lionel embraced her every bit as warmly as Thad had. "Of course not. We want you to be happy."

Veronica hugged Molly, too. She smoothed her hair with maternal affection, and consoled her compassionately, "Making mistakes is part of life. It's what you do afterward that counts. And it sounds to your father and me that you're doing your best to set things right."

Thad agreed with that. Errors happened. In hockey, in life. You still had to pick yourself up and go on. As he was trying to do.

When Thad was left alone with his mother after Lionel and Molly went to pick up dinner for the family, she looked at him knowingly. "Want to tell me what's going on with you?" she asked.

Thad figured he had to tell someone sometime. God knew it wasn't helping him to keep the heartbreak all to himself. Briefly, he explained the rift between him and Janey while his mother listened intently. "Well, what did you expect?" Veronica asked eventually, a lot less understanding about his situation than she had been about his younger sister's. She frowned at him disapprovingly. "I warned you not to come between a mother and her child."

Thad bristled at the unfair criticism. "I didn't do that."

Veronica scoffed as she got out dishes and began to set the table in the dining room. "I beg to disagree. I've seen the way Chris is now treating Janey. While it's still completely respectful, he's aloof in a way that's out of character!"

Thad felt a wave of guilt as he accepted a stack of napkins from his mother and set one at each place. "Because of me."

Veronica shrugged, as she carefully laid out the silverware. "I can't say why." She paused and looked Thad straight in the eye. "All I know is that since his injury Chris has shut down. And he doesn't seem to be bouncing back, the way any of us would have expected."

His mother's words stayed with Thad. He knew he had to talk to Chris. So he went to see Chris at the hospital during Chris's next physical therapy session, making sure he arrived at the end of his range-of-motion exercises with his physical therapist.

Thad held out an assisting hand as Chris got slowly down from the padded table. "How's it going?"

Chris winced as he landed on his feet and began making his way stiffly and painfully to the whirlpool. "How does it look?" he asked as he climbed in. "Lousy."

Thad lounged against the wall while the physical therapist set the timer and walked away, before continuing his probing. "Because you can't skate."

Chris leaned back against the rim, beginning to relax as the warm swirling water did its magic on his healing muscles. "Because my mom's unhappy again."

Thad did a double take. He had expected this to be all about Chris and his inability to play hockey right now. "I don't get it."

Chris shrugged his thin shoulders. Guilt flashed across his face.

For a second, Thad thought Chris wasn't going to answer him, then he finally admitted in a low, troubled voice, "She hasn't looked so scared and sad since my dad died." Chris shook his head, sighed remorsefully. "She didn't like my dad doing dangerous things, either. She always got mad when he went off to heli-ski in avalanche areas. But he did it anyway. Then when he didn't come back, she blamed herself. She said over and over she should've talked sense into him and made him stop. Just like she tried to talk sense into me about not playing hockey or going to camp this year."

Once again, Janey was taking too much on herself. And now her son was doing the same thing. Thad couldn't let it happen. "You thinking of giving up hockey?" he asked casually.

Chris's expression turned even bleaker. "I don't want to. It's the best thing in my life. But I don't want to make my mom miserable, either." Chris fell silent. Eyes shimmering, he went on in a low voice heavy with culpability, "She was crying when she came to the hospital the other day. Did you know that?"

Thad felt guilty, too—for not being able to accompany Chris to the hospital or be there with Janey to tell her the news about Chris's on-ice mishap. "I figured as much. But then, moms always cry when their kids get hurt. Even mine."

Chris's eyes widened in surprise. "But she's a physical therapist."

Thad grimaced as he thought about some of his own adventures in doctor's offices and physical rehab units. You didn't play a sport as tough and demanding as hockey without sustaining some injury, now and then. But that was just part of it. "And my mother gets scared and worried just like anyone else," Thad told Chris.

Chris took a moment to mull that over. "Did your mom ever try to get you to quit?"

"No." Thad smiled. "She always said when you love doing something—" or being with someone, Thad amended silently to himself "—it's always worth the extra effort."

"CAREFUL, CAREFUL," Janey said, as she and two other servers from The Wedding Inn set the wedding cake on the center of the antique mahogany dessert table.

"Beautiful, as always," Helen said, as she came up to stand beside Janey.

Janey sprinkled rose petals around the base of the cake, as the bride and groom had requested. She was no longer at a point in her life where she needed her mother's approval, but she always appreciated it. "I'm glad you think so."

"You've really outdone yourself lately, with the confections you've created," Helen continued, looking as pulled-together as always in a mint-green suit fit for the proprietress of the premiere wedding establishment in the central Carolina area.

"Thanks." Janey observed the basket-weave frosting from all angles, making sure it was still perfect.

"And while I'm happy you're succeeding—" Helen paused to lay out the sterling silver serving pieces, engraved with the happy couple's names "—I also wonder what is causing you to be so passionate and creative."

"Maybe I'm more focused," she said, as she added white satin ribbons around the edges of the layers to create an elegant appearance.

"And maybe you have a lot of emotional energy you don't know what to do with," Helen said as Janey artistically placed a few delicate blossoms over the top of the towering confection.

"Not that succeeding in business is a bad thing, mind you," Helen continued. "Just that I don't like to see you looking so…grim. And you have looked grim lately, Janey, despite all your success."

Finished, Janey straightened and did a final check of the cake. Satisfied all was in order for the cake-cutting ceremony later, she collected her things and moved away, fighting tears. Which was something that had been happening all too often in the days since Chris had gotten hurt.

"I don't think that's a surprise, Mom," Janey murmured as the two of them left the room and headed in the direction of Helen's office. "Thanks to all five of my brothers and Thad Lantz's interference, Chris is barely speaking to me."

Helen guided her inside her private haven, and closed the door behind them. "So talk to him," she encouraged, as sure as always that everything would work out if they only worked at it.

"I've tried." Janey placed a hand on the back of her neck and rubbed at the tense muscles. Usually she appreciated her mother's can-do attitude, but today it was only aggravating. "But he's acting just like Ty," she protested.

Helen surveyed her carefully. "Chris is reacting like any frustrated, injured athlete. And since you are the sister of a pro hockey player, you should know that."

"What are you trying to say to me?"

"I'm not saying anything. I'm asking. Are you in love with Thad Lantz?"

Janey folded her arms in front of her defensively. "What does it matter if I am?" She slumped down onto the sofa in the corner.

Helen perched on the edge of her desk. "So it wasn't just a fling the two of you were having."

"Not for me." Janey ran her hands through her hair, feeling more frustrated and discouraged than ever. "For him I was just a means to an end. To the family—the son—he's been wanting but didn't have." And knowing that just slayed her.

Helen scowled. "I don't believe that."

"Believe me, I didn't want to, either," Janey retorted, jumping to her feet once again. "But even when he proposed to me, Mom, he didn't mention love. Not once." And that had hurt, even when she told herself it didn't.

"And it's necessary for you to hear the words," Helen guessed.

Janey threw up her hands. "Well, duh."

"Showing you in every way that counts wasn't enough."

"How do you—?"

Helen smiled at her gently. "Because I saw the light in your eyes, and the smile on your face whenever you looked at him the night of his sister Molly's party here. I saw the spring in your step and your new outlook on life, and I knew he was responsible for bringing so much joy into your life, and Chris's, too."

Janey paused. "I thought you didn't approve of me seeing him." *I thought you were sure this was just another episode of recklessness and regret.*

Helen shrugged. "I admit I would have preferred a slower courtship but sometimes that isn't the way it happens. Sometimes feelings are fierce and true and so powerful there's no denying them."

That was how it happened. But it didn't mean there weren't obstacles standing in their way. "It's just such a bad time for me to be falling in love with someone," Janey ruminated, upset.

Helen scoffed. "Come on, Janey. You know there

is no orchestrating love. You can't just conjure it up on demand.''

"I don't see why not.'' She looked at her mother. "I want what you and Daddy had.''

Helen looked her in the eye. "Our life together wasn't perfect, honey.''

Janey pushed aside the suspicion she was being way too unrealistic yet again. "But you really loved each other.''

"Yes, we did. But that doesn't mean that our marriage wasn't without challenges,'' Helen corrected without an ounce of regret. "We got married awfully young and we had six children in nine years. Ed was on the road a lot with his job, which left a lot of the child-rearing to me.''

"But that was what you both wanted,'' Janey protested. "And the time was right.''

Helen leaned forward urgently. "Honey, that's another fallacy. The time is never right. There's never going to be a perfect time to fall in love or get married or have a baby. And if you wait for the perfect time, for everything to be just so, none of it will ever happen. If this is right, if you love Thad Lantz, or even think you do, you've got to take a risk and jump in with both feet.''

TAKE A RISK...take a risk... That was all Janey could think about as she headed home for the evening. When she got there, Chris was working hard on his math homework at the kitchen table. He had a pan of hot dogs simmering on the stove, a bowl of potato chips and some fruit cocktail with sliced bananas set out.

He looked up as she came in. For the first time since his injury, there was a smile on his face, contentment in his eyes. "I made dinner for us."

"So I see." Janey set down her shoulder bag and keys, feeling a little like she had landed in an alternate universe, the one that had existed before her son's quest to be an athlete had brought conflict and Thad Lantz into their lives. "You look happy," she said.

Chris put down his pencil. "Coach Lantz came to see me today during my physical therapy session." Chris regarded her steadily, sizing her up. "He said you weren't mad at me for getting hurt."

Janey blinked in a mixture of astonishment and dismay. "Of course I'm not angry with you!" She sat down opposite her son, knowing there was no better time to have a heart to heart. "What would ever make you think that?" she asked gently.

Chris shrugged. He flicked his thumb across the surface of his worksheet. "I dunno. I just got to thinking that maybe I was too much like Dad, and that I was—you know—" he stammered uncertainly "—making you unhappy with all my 'risky behavior.'"

Hearing the exact words she had used to describe Ty's actions during one of their many fights on the subject, filled Janey with guilt. They hadn't meant for Chris to hear them arguing. Obviously, he had. And that had scarred him as deeply as Ty's reckless pursuits and senseless death. The last thing she had ever wanted was for Chris to feel like he had let her down in the same way, when the truth was he had done nothing of the sort. "Listen to me, Chris. Playing hockey is not risky."

He lifted a skeptical brow and slumped back in his chair. "Kids get hurt all the time."

Janey shrugged in a way that let him know she had finally come to terms with his athletic ambitions. "Kids get hurt riding skateboards and you do that, too."

Chris flashed a crooked smile. "So you don't mind?"

Janey reached over and patted his arm affectionately. "I want you to go for your dreams, whatever they are." She looked at him sincerely. "I will support you."

Chris gulped, his features once again taking on the pinched, anxious look. "But if you get scared—"

Janey lifted a silencing palm. "You don't have to be concerned about me fretting. Mothers fret all the time—it's our prerogative. If it weren't hockey, it would just be something else I'd be agonizing over. Like math."

"You don't have to worry about that," Chris reassured her. "I asked my teacher for extra help today after summer school and she gave it to me. She'd have done it before—I just never asked her before. Because I didn't want to look like a nerd. But Coach made me see that asking for what you need is never something to be ashamed of. It's the not asking, the not going after what you want that causes problems in people's lives.''

INDEED, JANEY THOUGHT, all that evening and well into the next business day. The trouble was, she knew what she wanted. Had realized it all along, even when she was protesting a little too much. So the only thing to do was swallow her pride, and hope like heck it wasn't too late to undo the damage she had done in kicking Thad Lantz out of her life. But first she had an appointment at the arena in Raleigh, with the Storm business management team. They wanted to photograph the cakes and cupcakes being offered in the new birthday celebration ticket packages.

Leaving her new employee—an experienced pastry chef she had hired yesterday to help her with the additional business—to close up the bakery, she loaded everything into her car and proceeded to the arena, arriving some twenty minutes ahead of schedule.

The building was closed to the public, but the guards were expecting her and waved her on up to the executive offices. Janey was just getting off the escalator when she saw Thad at the other end of the carpeted hall. If he was surprised to see her, he didn't show it. Just kind of nodded and kept going in the opposite direction.

Swallowing her disappointment, Janey proceeded with her business. The photography session with the team mascot went as smoothly as she had hoped. An hour later, Janey was walking back to the escalator, wondering if Thad was still around, or if she should just wait and track him down at his home. Assuming, of course, that he would see her. She had been awfully rough on him.

"Mrs. Hart Campbell?" The security guard who had allowed her inside was suddenly standing in front of her, blocking her way. "If you don't mind, we'd like you to leave another way."

Well, there went her chances of making amends with Thad now, Janey thought with a sigh. She smiled graciously at the guard, aware he was just doing his job. "Certainly."

He led her down the hall, through a set of doors marked Employees Only, down three flights of stairs, and yet another hall, to a cement floored area that led out onto the home team's bench in the brightly lit arena. Janey turned, disquieted. The security guard merely smiled and pointed to the other end of the bench, behind the protective glass. "Coach Lantz wants a word with you," the guard said. He smiled and left as discreetly as he had appeared.

Her heart racing, Janey turned to face the man who had swiftly become the love of her life. Stunned by how hungry she was for the sight of him, after just a week apart, she let her eyes rove over him. He was wearing a red-and-gray polo shirt with the Storm emblem on the chest, jeans that encased his long, sturdy legs. And he had never looked more ruggedly handsome or determined.

As he moved toward her, the arena lights dimmed to a romantic hue. "If I didn't know better, I'd think you were trying to get cozy with me,'' Janey quipped, knowing she would like nothing better.

Thad looked down at her, his electric-blue eyes somber. ''Would that be such a bad thing?'' he asked softly.

Suddenly, Janey had a lump in her throat, and a smidgen of much-needed hope growing deep inside her. Love took work. It didn't happen without sacrifice. She knew that now. And the first thing to go was going to be her pride. ''Oh, Thad, I'm so sorry,'' she whispered, taking both his hands in hers and clasping them tightly.

His callused palms gripped hers. ''So am I,'' he told her huskily.

''You were right.'' Now that they were face-to-face again, she couldn't get the words out fast enough. ''I was afraid to put my heart on the line.'' Afraid to love. Afraid to risk. Afraid to change.

He let go of her hands, wrapped his arms around her back and guided her near, until they collided, hardness to softness. He looked down at her intensely. ''And now?'' he asked, so softly she had to strain to hear.

Janey luxuriated in the comfort of his warm embrace and the potent resolve on his face. ''I realize I'm never going to be happy unless I go after what I want,'' she whispered as tears of happiness welled up behind her eyes.

''Which is—?''

''What you want.'' And had been, unlike her, unafraid to pursue. "A family," she whispered emotionally. "With you and me and Chris."

For the first time, caution warred with the determination on his face. "I want a heck of a lot more than that with you, Janey," he told her seriously, all the tenderness she had ever dreamed of radiating in his low voice. He tucked one hand beneath her chin, lifting her face to his. With the other, he tightened his grip on her possessively. "I want you to love me the way I love you, with all my heart and soul."

Janey blinked. "What did you just say?" she asked as her heart turned somersaults in her chest.

Thad looked deep into her eyes, more than happy to repeat the words again. "That I love you."

Happiness bubbled up inside her as all her dreams came true, Janey wreathed her arms around him. "I love you, too," she said in a choked up voice. "So very much."

He studied her, curious now, needing to understand her as much as she yearned to know the innermost parts of him. "Why do you look so surprised?"

"Because," Janey shrugged, embarrassed, "you never said."

"I didn't think I had to. I thought I showed you how I felt every time I held you, kissed you, made love with you."

And he had, Janey thought. She just hadn't trusted it. Hadn't trusted herself. Or the love she was feeling for him.

He gently stroked her hair as he looked down at her as if she were the most wonderful woman on earth. "Is that why you turned down my marriage proposal?" he asked curiously.

Janey rose up on tiptoe and kissed his cheek, admitting. "That and because I was scared you wouldn't stay as attracted to me as you are right now."

Thad grinned wickedly. He bent his head and kissed her until her senses flamed and the world spun around them. "Not much chance of that," he murmured sexily, as they continued to kiss, sweetly, passionately, with all the love in their hearts. Both were trembling as they drew apart.

But Janey knew there were things she had to make plain, if they wanted to be happy in the long run. "I want this to last, Thad." She ran her fingers through his dark hair and gazed into his eyes. "If we're going to do it, I want us to commit ourselves heart and soul to the relationship. I want it to be for real, forever." Her voice caught huskily. "I want Chris to know he can count on our devotion to each other as much as he can count on us to be there for him."

"You have my word of honor, Janey," Thad told her hoarsely. "I'm not just in this for the short haul. And to prove it to you—" He turned, gave the thumbs up.

Suddenly the Jumbotron that hung above center ice came on.

The screens flashed film of referees in zebra-striped uniforms making Misconduct and then Time-Out signs.

"So what's it going to be?" Thad probed as the

referees on the screen mimed the signs for Delay Of Game and Holding.

"This?" Thad asked as the referees gestured a triumphant Goal Scored.

"Or this?" Thad continued as they slashed the Wash Out, or No Goal sign.

Laughing at the unique way he had fashioned his proposal, Janey wrapped her arms about his neck, stood on tiptoe, and kissed him with all the love and passion she possessed, until both of them were aching for more. "Coach," she said happily. "You just won the game."

*   *   *   *   *

In September 2005 Silhouette Special Edition presents the third instalment in Cathy Gillen Thacker's captivating mini-series

THE BRIDES OF HOLLY SPRINGS.

Turn the page for a sneak preview of
The Secret Seduction
—Fletcher Hart's story!

The Secret Seduction
by
Cathy Gillen Thacker

Honestly, Lily Madsen thought as she watched the disheveled "cowboy" climb down from the truck, that man in the snug-fitting jeans, chambray shirt and boots was enough to take your breath away. Or he would have been, she amended silently to herself, if he hadn't been Fletcher Hart. The most reckless and restless of Helen Hart's five sons, the thirty-year-old Fletcher had a reputation for loving and leaving women, and never committing to much of anything—save his thriving Holly Springs, North Carolina, vet practice—for long.

"Why are you being so all-fired difficult?" Lily glared at him and continued the conversation the two of them had started before Fletcher had cut it short and headed off on an emergency call on a nearby farm. "All I am asking for is a simple introduction to Carson McRue. I'll take it the rest of the way."

Fletcher slanted her a deeply cynical look, followed it with a way too knowing half smile, then strode toward the back door of the clinic. "The answer is still no, Lily."

Simmering with a mixture of resentment, anger and another emotion she couldn't quite identify, Lily followed Fletcher into the building, aware that unlike the building, which smelled quite antiseptic, he smelled like he had been rolling around in the back of a barn. And perhaps he had been, she thought, noting the sweat stains on his shirt, the mud clinging to his sculpted body.

Oblivious to her scrutiny of him, he walked purposefully into a glass-walled room. On the other side of the partition were an assortment of cats and dogs in metal cages. All appeared to be recovering from operations or illnesses and were resting comfortably.

On their side of the glass wall, there was another large crate with a dog inside who did not appear to have had surgery.

Lily watched as Fletcher hunkered down beside the crate and peered in. To her frustration, he seemed a lot more interested in his canine patient than what she had to say to him.

Hands on her hips, she demanded with all the authority she could muster, "Just what is your objection to my meeting the man anyway?"

Fletcher paused to give a comforting pat to an ailing yellow lab, who looked up at him with big sad eyes, before straightening once again. "Besides the fact that he's an egotistical TV star who doesn't care about anyone but himself, you mean?"

Lily huffed her exasperation, and trying all the

while not to notice how soft and touchable Fletcher's shaggy honey-brown hair was, how sexy his golden brown eyes. Honestly, you would think the way Fletcher acted that he was the star of a hit TV show, instead of a local vet who was—as always—in need of a haircut. Just because he had a masculinely chiseled face, with the don't-mess-with-me Hart jaw, expressive, kissable lips, very strong nose and even more well-defined cheekbones, did not mean that she had to swoon at his feet. Or dream of being taken in by his powerful, six-foot-one frame, with the broad shoulders, impossibly solid chest and long, muscular legs.

"Just because Carson McRue is rich and famous—"

Fletcher headed up the stairs that led to his apartment on the second floor, unbuttoning his filthy shirt as he went. "Let's just cut the bull, shall we?"

"I don't—"

He stopped at the top of the stairs and stripped off his shirt, leaving Lily with a bird's-eye view of lots of satiny-smooth male skin, a T-shaped mat of golden brown hair, and six-pack abs to die for. With effort, she dragged her glance away before she could really give in to temptation and slide her glance lower.

Oblivious to the licentious direction of her thoughts, Fletcher continued mocking her. "I know about the bet you made with all your friends. Okay, Lily? Everyone in town does."

While Fletcher watched, embarrassed color crept to her cheeks. Lily gulped her dismay. She never should have indulged in such bold talk at her birthday party last week. But then she never should have let her friends talk her into having not just one but two margaritas with her enchiladas, either. Everyone knew she couldn't hold her liquor.

Forcing herself to meet Fletcher's boldly assessing gaze head-on, Lily demanded archly, "Who told you?"

"That you've promised when Carson McRue's private jet leaves Carolina, you're going to be on it?" Fletcher picked up where Lily left off. "Well, let's see. There's my sister, Janey. My brother Joe's wife, Emma. Hannah Reid, over at Classic Car Auto Repair. And everyone else who heard you swear that you could get a hot date with the dim bulb in just one week."

Fletcher Hart knew everything, all right. Except of course what had prompted Lily to make such an unlikely, hedonistic boast in the first place. She pushed her rebuttal through gritted teeth. "Carson McRue is not a dim bulb. Or an egotistical star."

That cynical smile again. "And how would you know this?" Fletcher challenged as he unlocked the door, strode into his apartment and headed to the bathroom at the rear.

Lily had the choice of following or cooling her heels. She knew what he would have preferred, so she did the exact opposite. Pulse racing, she leaned against the hallway wall and continued their conversation as nonchalantly as if she did things this crazily intimate with men she barely knew every single day.

"I know because I've watched his TV show every week for the last five years." The action-adventure show about an easygoing Hollywood private eye had been the one bright spot in many a stressful week. Lily had watched it in hospital rooms, and waiting rooms, as well as at home. And it had never failed to make her forget her problems, at least temporarily. Right now, she needed to forget her problems.

Fletcher kicked off one boot, then the other. "Carson McRue plays a character, Lily. What you see on TV is all an act, albeit a highly polished one."

"I know that," Lily retorted, just as drolly, as she heard a zip, and a whoosh of fabric, and *was that the shower starting?* "But no one could actually pretend to be that caring and compassionate." At least Lily hoped that was the case. Otherwise, her goose was cooked. She would never be able to live down this drunken boast.

"Doesn't matter." The shower curtain opened and closed. Water pelted in an entirely different rhythm and the aroma of soap and shampoo and...man... wafted out on the steamy air as Fletcher scrubbed himself clean. "I'm still not introducing you to him." He spoke above the din of the running water.

At Fletcher's stubbornness, it was all Lily could do not to stomp her foot. "But he and the rest of the show's cast and crew will be here tomorrow," she protested hotly as the water shut off, the shower curtain pulled open with a telltale whoosh, and a towel was ripped off the rack with equal carelessness. "And you're the only one in town who has met him."

Six heavy male footsteps later, Fletcher was standing in the hall. Knowing she would be a coward if she didn't look, Lily opened her eyes and she was rendered speechless. Fletcher was standing there, regarding her curiously and unabashedly. He had a towel slung low around his waist. He was using another on his hair. And, she noticed disconcertingly, he looked every bit as deliciously sexy wet as he did dry....

Don't forget
The Secret Seduction
is available in September 2005.

SILHOUETTE®

SPECIAL EDITION™

THE SECRET SEDUCTION Cathy Gillen Thacker

The Brides of Holly Springs

Innocent Lily Madsen outrages wickedly gorgeous Fletcher Hart when he hears that she's bet she can get a date with a visiting TV celebrity. The cynical vet is determined to interfere in all her plans *personally!*

THE PRINCE'S BRIDE Lois Faye Dyer

The Parks Empire

Wedding planner Emily Parks had decided to focus on her career. She never imagined that the dashing Prince Lazhar Eban would ever want her to be his bride, and she didn't know that a business proposition had prompted his proposal!

THE STRONG SILENT TYPE Marie Ferrarella

Cavanaugh Justice

He wasn't much on conversation. But police officer Teri Cavanaugh's new partner, Jack Hawkins, was really easy on the eyes. Teri resolved to get to know Hawk and she couldn't help but fall for the man he revealed himself to be...

THE BABY THEY BOTH LOVED Nikki Benjamin

When writer Simon Gilmore discovered a son he never knew was his, he had to fight the child's legal guardian, green-eyed waitress Kit Davenport, for custody. Would the baby they both loved make enemies become a loving family?

WRONG TWIN, RIGHT MAN Laurie Campbell

Beth Montoya and her husband, Rafael, were not happy when Beth was in a tragic accident. All Rafael could do was offer to take care of Anne, Beth's surviving twin, while she recovered. Then passion flared between them...

BABIES IN THE BARGAIN Victoria Pade

Northbridge Nuptials

After Kira Wentworth's sister was killed, she insisted on taking care of the twin toddlers left behind. But when she got to know the girls' father, injured hero cop Cutler Grant, she found herself bargaining for more than just the babies!

Don't miss out! On sale from 19th August 2005

Available at most branches of WHSmith, Tesco, ASDA, Borders, Eason, Sainsbury's and most bookshops

Visit our website at www.silhouette.co.uk

SILHOUETTE®

SPECIAL EDITION™

CATHY GILLEN
THACKER

presents her captivating new series

The Brides of Holly Springs

Weddings are serious business in the picturesque
town of Holly Springs! Helen Hart, no-nonsense
steel magnolia, has single-handedly raised five
sons and one feisty daughter and is looking to
see her children married!

The Virgin's Secret Marriage
July 2005

The Secret Wedding Wish
August 2005

The Secret Seduction
September 2005

Plain Jane's Secret Life
October 2005

Desert Heat

Susan Mallery
Alexandra Sellers

On sale 19th August 2005

Available at most branches of WHSmith, Tesco, ASDA, Martins, Borders, Eason, Sainsbury's and all good paperback bookshops.

ANN HAVEN

PEGGY NICHOLSON

Homeward
Bound

Because when baby's on the way

there's no place like home...

On sale 19th August 2005

Available at most branches of WHSmith, Tesco, ASDA, Borders, Eason, Sainsbury's and most bookshops.

FREE

4 BOOKS AND A SURPRISE GIFT!

We would like to take this opportunity to thank you for reading this Silhouette® book by offering you the chance to take FOUR more specially selected titles from the Special Edition™ series absolutely FREE! We're also making this offer to introduce you to the benefits of the Reader Service™—

- ★ **FREE home delivery**
- ★ **FREE gifts and competitions**
- ★ **FREE monthly Newsletter**
- ★ **Books available before they're in the shops**
- ★ **Exclusive Reader Service offers**

Accepting these FREE books and gift places you under no obligation to buy; you may cancel at any time, even after receiving your free shipment. Simply complete your details below and return the entire page to the address below. You don't even need a stamp!

YES! Please send me 4 free Special Edition books and a surprise gift. I understand that unless you hear from me, I will receive 6 superb new titles every month for just £3.05 each, postage and packing free. I am under no obligation to purchase any books and may cancel my subscription at any time. The free books and gift will be mine to keep in any case.

E5ZEE

Ms/Mrs/Miss/Mr...Initials ....

BLOCK CAPITALS PLEASE

Surname ....

Address ....

....

....Postcode ....

Send this whole page to:
The Reader Service, FREEPOST CN81, Croydon, CR9 3WZ